the

unexpected

connection

REBECCA BRANCH

The Unexpected Connection

Trilogy Christian Publishers
A Wholly Owned Subsidiary of Trinity Broadcasting Network
2442 Michelle Drive, Tustin, CA 92780

Rights Department, 2442 Michelle Drive, Tustin, CA 92780.

Trilogy Christian Publishing/TBN and colophon are trademarks of Trinity Broadcasting Network.

Cover design by Nicole McDaniel

For information about special discounts for bulk purchases, please contact Trilogy Christian Publishing.

Trilogy Disclaimer: The views and content expressed in this book are those of the author and may not necessarily reflect the views and doctrine of Trilogy Christian Publishing or the Trinity Broadcasting Network.

Manufactured in the United States of America
10 9 8 7 6 5 4 3 2 1
Library of Congress Cataloging-in-Publication Data is available.

ISBN: 979-8-88738-429-0
E-ISBN: 979-8-88738-430-6

acknowledgments

For my Lord and Savior Jesus Christ. Your love is unfathomable. Your compassion is breathtaking. Your sacrifice is immeasurable. Thank You for the cross and for bridging the gap between us and God. This heart is forever Yours.

Thank You, Father God, for this beautiful life. Thank You for this beautiful creation. Thank You for giving Your Son as the atoning sacrifice for our sins and giving us a way back to You. Time and again, You display Your heart to us in the Bible, and it is something we constantly glean more understanding about. May the work of my hands and the work of my heart be pleasing in Your sight. Thank You for the uniqueness and precision of prophecy.

Holy Spirit, giver of love, joy, peace, longsuffering, kindness, goodness, faithfulness, gentleness, and self-control. Holy Spirit, giver of wisdom, knowledge, faith, healings, miracles, prophecy, discerning of spirits, different kinds of tongues, and interpretation of tongues, may we feel an abundance of Your presence pour out as our need for You is so great in this hour.

To my family, thank you for every part of this shared experience of life. We have seen God move in some exceptionally remarkable ways, and suffice it to say we will continue to see Him move in even more remarkable ways. What great days these will be. I love you all more than I can adequately express with words.

table of contents

prologue

Prophecy is an interesting thing. Both mysterious and deeply revealing. Something that manifests in various ways. It is oftentimes unexpected but always needed. It is uniquely dynamic. It holds the authority of heaven and the compassion of the cross of Christ. It is predictive, yes, but it is infinitely more than that.

Much like love that has the unique ability to transcend both time and space, prophecy continually defies the limitations of the natural world. Instead, prophecy introduces the natural world to the unseen things of God, Jesus Christ, and the Holy Spirit. Prophecy has unfettered access to all the storerooms of heaven, and it springs forward like wells of living water pouring out from the throne of the Father.

Prophecy is so all-encompassing that it impacts the broadest things to the most detailed and intricate things. From the shaping of the universe to the most subtle and nuanced events that happen in a person's life, prophecy is that all-encompassing. From the galaxies that spin around consistently putting on display the intelligent and divine design of the universe to the broken pieces of a heart desperate for the intervention of God in its life. Prophecy reflects the authority of God, the power of God, and the love of God with such detail that when it is truly understood, it fills the heart with a sense of wonder and awe at the complex and beautiful displays of the heart of the Father toward His creation.

It is immersed within the mysteries of prophecy where this story begins.

the wilderness

Bring Back the Erring One

*Brethren, if anyone among you wanders from the truth,
and someone turns him back, let him know that he who
turns a sinner from the error of his way will save a soul
from death and cover a multitude of sins.*

— James 5:19–20 (NKJV)

Aria

I walked out of the movie theater in a daze. I had spent the past several months feeling numb within my soul. As I absentmindedly put one foot in front of another, I sensed the numbness was lifting.

I knew there was more to life than the constant cycles of pain and brokenness. The Lord had demonstrated that to me on so many occasions, but this season was unquestionably a dry one for my soul.

I wanted to help others, but how could I when my soul was in such despair?

I pondered on the events of the film I had just watched as I drove home from the theater. There was a shift taking place inside of me, a marker of the Lord beginning a work in my life.

I sighed.

I knew it would take some time for the work the Lord was doing to begin to truly manifest, but the markers of His work were unquestionably evident. I knew this feeling well. It was a deep sense of knowing that when the haze over my mind was being shifted, it would demonstrate the move of the Lord in my life.

I briefly wondered if this would also mean the dreams would begin again.

I knew that dreams were a tool the Lord used to communicate to His children, but I also knew not to depend on dreams as the only way to hear from God. There were so many ways the Lord could speak to His children. Dreams were simply and profoundly one of the strongest instruments of communication the Lord would use in my life.

These days, I didn't dream much.

In a dry season such as this one, I found that I deeply missed those dreams. I missed the prophetic symbolism of those dreams. I missed searching out the meaning and finding prophetic instruction inside those night parables the Lord gave me.

It felt like I wasn't hearing from the Lord. It became more difficult with each passing day to enter into prayer time with Him. I knew this was a wilderness season. It bore all the markers of exactly that, with the pressures mounting from all around me.

I parked my car as I arrived home. The cold December air met me with its startling touch against my cheeks. I took a deep breath as I closed the car door and paused to look up at the clear night sky. The cool air pierced my lungs as I embraced the opportunity to gaze at the stars lighting up the darkness of night.

I found peace every time I looked at those stars. The powerful reality that God designed the complexities of such a vast universe that I couldn't understand always served to humble me. It reminded me that there was more than just this wilderness season that dominated so much of my attention.

It never ceased to amaze me how taking a few precious moments to take in the vastness of God's creation could completely expel the ever-present components of the wilderness I was in. What a demonstration of God's power; to cast away the burdens on a soul with the stunning display of a clear night sky.

I was thankful for these stolen moments of peace.

This wasn't my first wilderness season. As much as I did not like them, I knew from first-hand experience that God would use them for spiritual growth within me. Each one of those seasons was uniquely designed to address roots that God no longer wanted to be so deeply immersed in the soil of my life.

He knew me well.

I never chose these seasons. They were not fun to be immersed in. They required patience and trust in the Lord. They required perseverance, as one of the dominant components of these times, to confront fear.

I lingered for a while still as I fought against the cold night air so I could gaze up at those stars for a few more precious moments. Tomorrow would have an unreasonable amount of expectations from me. It would demand things from me that would test the resolve of my spirit. It would test my walk as a Christian. Day after day, my soul suffered blow after blow.

If I had tears left to cry, I would cry those tears in this moment.

There'd been so much saturation of wickedness everywhere lately. I knew that it would be like this in the last days Jesus warned about, but being inside of it was much more difficult than I had expected it to be. I needed the Lord more and more these days because it felt like every place that I turned, I saw the advancement of the enemy.

I needed the advancement of God.

I wanted to pray. I wanted so much to connect to God, but my soul hurt so much from seeing the pain inflicted upon the world from the wickedness that abounded that I couldn't find the words to say to God.

Even though I knew this was not how this worked, I still wanted this wilderness season to be over and done with. I didn't want to carry this burden anymore. It was crushing me.

That's why I started to feel so numb. Feeling numb had become like a defense mechanism; the only thing I had to fall back on at the moment. Whatever it was that God was doing, I needed Him to do it quickly because I did not like being in this spiritually barren place.

I thought about the movie I had just left and the un-mistakable markers of the numbness lifting. There was a part of me that battled the fear of what it would mean to have the numbness leave me. It had felt like so long that the numbness had been my fraudulent security blanket. What would I do without it if God was indeed moving? It made sense that the first move God would have to make would be to put something in my path that would remove that security blanket of numbness away from me.

What was it about the film that had been enough to shake me so gently?

That was a question I would ponder on over the course of the next few weeks. The battles remained, but now there was the added component of God moving and shaking me awake. He clearly didn't want me relying on the numbness anymore. He wanted me to feel what was taking place around me. I fought against it because it was a difficult thing to be an empathetic person in a world that was hurting and lashing out with rage because of that hurt and pain.

I knew the Father well enough to know that He didn't want me to suffer alongside others who were suffering. If all everyone did was suffer, then how would that cycle be broken? God needed people to stand in the gap to help alleviate the pain. He didn't want people to stay prisoners of pain. He wanted to show people the path to true freedom.

There had to be a remnant of God's children ready to stand in the gap to point people to Christ and His love and gift of salvation.

While driving one morning, I broke down and cried. I asked the Lord to help me. I told Him I couldn't stay in this barren spiritual place any longer. I patched myself up, feeling a lot like I was holding the pieces of myself together in everything I did. I wanted so much to be free from this spiritual destitution. I knew there was so much more to life than this. Knowing that made this wilderness season difficult in such a disturbingly unique way.

The answer hit me one night while I was still meditating on the film and why it had impacted me the way it did. The Holy Spirit had kept bringing it into my awareness over the course of the past few weeks, and I knew well enough by now that anytime the Holy Spirit moved in such a way, I needed to be sensitive to why it was happening.

Redemption.

I saw the markers of redemption in the storyline of one of the characters. It was the pain in his eyes that had originally caught my attention. As the empathetic person God had developed me into, I was always inextricably drawn to the markers of pain evident in a person's eyes.

I had become well acquainted with the way pain reflected itself within the depths of the eyes.

Deep in my spirit, I had a sense that this person was not simply acting a part in the storyline they represented. He seemed to be drawing from his own experience with pain. With the current state of the world being what it was, with such anger and animosity and infliction of pain, it was like a healing balm being splashed on my soul as the realization finally birthed itself inside of me that the reason why this film would not leave my awareness was because of that beautiful symbolism of redemption immersed within the storyline and the evidence of the actor's acquaintance with pain so clearly displayed in his eyes.

And all it took was a few brief moments of onscreen portrayal to get a huge message across to whoever was willing enough to look for it and sensitive enough to see it. After seeing so much anger and hatred everywhere I turned, it was inexplicably beautiful to be able to catch this glimpse of something as profoundly beautiful as redemption. I was like a woman dying of thirst in a barren wasteland that was suddenly revived by wells of living water pouring straight from the throne of God.

I found myself immediately grateful to God for shining this light in the darkness of my night. As a born-again Christian, I knew redemption well. I had been saved for twelve years and experienced so many beautiful layers of redemption that all began with asking Jesus Christ into my life as my Lord and Savior.

But God wasn't finished. Not by a long shot.

While the upheaval in the spiritual realm continued to amplify and pour over into the physical reality of our world, the Lord led me on a path out of my wilderness. It didn't take long for me to discover that this actor's pain was not only very real, but it was of spiritual origins. I found myself stunned to discover that he knew of Jesus.

Reflections of Christ were evidenced in the way he spoke. Reflections of Christ were evidenced in his humility and self-awareness. Reflections of Christ were evidenced in his kindness and his deep intuition. He openly admitted he had a relationship with Christ.

Like the world's largest dam finally caving to the pressure of the water mounting against its concrete infostructure, the spiritual dam inside of me finally gave to the pressure that had continually mounted against me. I found myself completely shattered as I drove one morning. I cried like my world was ending, and though my world was not ending, deep down, I knew my wilderness season was.

I gazed at the early morning winter sky as I thanked God over and over because that was all I knew how to do. The tears fell of their own volition. I was speechless and in awe and wonder at how magnificent God was. All I needed to see inside the constant barrage of pressure and pain and anger was one ray of hope. One reflection of Christ in a world that was so quickly becoming lost because it didn't know Christ. Just one moment of one eternally fundamental spiritual truth that would always outshine the greatest darkness in existence.

That darkness had been trying to crush me with its oppression and lies, and here God was, caring so much about the plight of my spirit that He gave me this little ray of sunshine and knew it would be powerful enough to dispel the oppression of that darkness.

I knew my face would be swollen and red from the rapid cascade of tears that finally broke free from the confines of my eyes. I knew I would see the curiosity in the eyes of the public as they saw the evidence of the emotional battle so clearly displayed on my face. I knew people would wonder.

But I also knew that no one would ask me questions. They never did.

Deep down, I longed for a world free from the influence of the enemy, but I knew that time had not yet arrived. People would continue on as they battled their own battles. Manifestations of their pain would be evident on their faces. Could I come back to the place where I may be able to help ease a burden here and there for those whose eyes were down cast and whose shoulders slumped with the invisible weight they carried upon their shoulders?

That was my hope; to get back to that place where I could help others ease their burden, overcome their battles, and connect them to the only one in whom they could find eternal redemption. Jesus Christ is the answer to sin, and I wanted to help people find Him. God said it was His will that none would perish and that all would come to know Him. I consider it to be one of the greatest blessings and honors to be able to serve the Lord and others by helping people find salvation and experience the love of God firsthand.

the call

I stared at the words on the screen of my computer. I gazed at the writing on the word document with wide eyes. I had originally meant to write a thank you letter to the actor for something that had a much larger impact on my spiritual walk than I could ever adequately convey.

But I still wanted to try to convey that sentiment.

After a week of trying to find the right words to say to attempt to communicate my gratitude, I was surprised by what had come out of me and onto that blank screen waiting patiently to be written upon. This was not at all what I had originally thought it would be. But, as I assessed the words on the screen, I knew it was what it was supposed to be. This wasn't the first time I aimed for something, and the Holy Spirit had other plans. I had learned quickly that His plans were always the best to follow.

With thoughtful deliberation, I reviewed some parts of the letter I knew I was going to send, but at this time, I had no clue how I was going to get it to the person.

The reality of living a life and battling the temptations of the lust of the flesh, the lust of the eyes, and the pride of

life is that a person who is after the deepest truth of ex-
istence inevitably finds themselves in a brutal contention
for the truth. It is a war that takes place in the very center
of who we are. It shakes up the foundation of our soul. It
awakens our spirit. And it is a fight that must take place
on a battlefield of destruction where it is just you faced
with a true existential crisis. It ends up becoming a season
in which you are about as far away from being okay as
you can possibly be. Then again, being okay is a matter
of personal interpretation when reflecting on the current
condition of our soul. Our perception of being okay
may not necessarily accurately reflect the truth of what
it means to be okay. And though it does not feel good to
be in that place, the end result is designed to bring about
true freedom.

What are we fighting for? Is it surviving in the hopes
of sustaining a body that was never meant to be eternal?
Or are we fighting for an eternity that will ensure true
survival?

I paused as I thought about what God was up to. This
was very different from the letter of gratitude I had originally wanted to send. I scanned the letter further.

When we strike another down, we lose a part of
ourselves.

We are designed to love and create. So then, it's natural for the soul (our mind, our will, and our emotions) to grieve when we do not embrace these things. It is natural for the soul to grieve when we operate against these things. I would take that one step further and say it has been my bittersweet experience that these things do indeed grieve the soul, but they devastate the spirit. It has certainly devastated mine just witnessing it. Bittersweet indeed. Bitter because of the consequences of these things. Sweet because it is quite effective in teaching the lesson that every single thing we do matters well beyond what we think it does.

Where does this leave a lost and broken world full of hurting people?

It will all amplify, both the good things and the bad things, as the pressure continues to mount. As the pressure mounts, events will happen quicker. There's a natural amplification process, after all. People must contend with themselves, though there will probably be too many who will contend with others instead. It has become too easy for this world to inflict pain on others without thought or care for the damage being done to both themselves and the person they inflict the pain upon. It's like the conscious mind of so many has been seared. I'd like to think that the seared conscious of an individual can be healed, but the real question becomes: how? If we give no thought or care to giving love or care or affection to others, then it is reasonable to question if we ourselves have what it takes to help another person heal.

Was this really the letter the Lord would have me send?

Justice without love and hope can quickly turn into retribution, and retribution leaves despair in its wake.

It is the deepest desire of my heart for people to find the answer to the pain. For people to know where true hope can be found. It is the deepest desire of my heart for people to find true healing. I sincerely believe that if people truly understood who Jesus is and what His will is in all of this, they would run to Him to be embraced by Him. Perhaps that is the hope in me rising to the surface. Perhaps, I just think that way because that has been His impact on me. Though I won't presume to know Him fully, I am looking forward to spending my existence searching out every facet of who He is.

On the other side of this, we will come to a true understanding of the consequences of our lives. I pray that I can stand before Christ when the time has finally arrived with some semblance of grace and true humility because I know how much I have failed. And I know that the ways in which I have achieved success by His standards are rewards that belong to Him alone, as they should. Until then, I embrace that unspeakably beautiful cross and hope and plead with the Lord to hasten in His return, and I do this out of the desperation of my own heart.

I wrote what I am about to share when I was in a season of intense pain. There was one day in particular that was too much for me to walk through on my own. So, I wrote something where I tried to feel the intensity and the magnitude of what Jesus did in the Garden of Gethsemane. This poem is what the result was.

I'm in the Garden with Jesus,
looking into His eyes as He asks the Father
    that, if it is possible, let this cup pass from
    Him.
I'm in the Garden with Jesus,
face to face kneeling before Him and watch-
    ing Him sweat blood as He willingly takes
    on my sin to save me, and His body bares
    the exertion that comes with carrying the
    weight of sin.
I'm in the Garden with Jesus,
right there with Him as He takes the first
    steps that put Him right on the path to the
    cross of the salvation of all mankind.
My sin follows Him with each step He takes.
My sin stands before Him as He is beaten
    because of who He is.
He takes each beating for me.
I'm with Jesus as He is taunted, tormented,
    and scourged, all so that I might be saved.

I'm with Jesus,

right there alongside Him as He carries the
cross that He has chosen to die upon for
me.

I'm the spectator who watches the nails
driven into His righteous flesh.

I'm with Jesus,

standing before the cross He is nailed upon.

I'm with Jesus,

as every drop of blood leaves His body.

I'm with Jesus,

as He breathes His last breath and dies an
undeserving death, a death that I deserve.

Jesus is with me,

in the accident.

Jesus is with me,

in the ambulance.

Jesus is with me,

in the hospital bed.

Jesus is with me in my pain.

I'm with Jesus in the Garden,

as He bares my sin for me because He loves
me so much He won't let me be without
Him.

I'm with Jesus in the Garden,

as He gives me the greatest gift I will ever be
given.

A gift whose value is beyond measure.

I'm with Jesus in the Garden,

looking into His eyes, I feel the complete-
ness and the enormity of His love and

know that He has sacrificed and paid it all
for me.
You are in the Garden with Jesus.

*When I think of my Lord and Savior, the word
"relationship" doesn't seem to be able to encompass what
He is to me. I belong to Him. He has never terrified me.
I have never found myself intimidated by His divinity. It
has always been the opposite for me. He is my home in
the truest sense of what home is. Even more than that,
somehow. He overwhelms me, and I find I long to be
overwhelmed by Him. He's not unreachable to me. I am
inexplicably intertwined with Him.*

*When I have truly succeeded in deconstructing
myself, I find oneness with Him. Is there any deeper level
of trust than this that can be obtained?*

I didn't always know Him. But He always knew me.

*I will close by saying, take from this what you will. It
is given with the purest of intentions. It is my hope that
you might draw from this what matters most.*

Your friend in faith.

If this person understood Jesus the way I suspected
he did, then I imagined this would convey quite well the
message the Lord wanted it to convey. I wondered why it
was the Holy Spirit had led me in this direction instead
of the expression of my gratitude.

As it turned out, it didn't take long for me to find out why the Holy Spirit led me in this direction instead. I didn't sign my name on the letter, and I didn't put my return address. I put the information in a post office box the Lord led me to open and proceeded to inquire of the Lord as to how to get this letter delivered to this person. It wasn't as simple as searching Google for mailing address information. Yet, I knew that if this was something that was indeed orchestrated by the Lord, He would make a way.

Shortly thereafter, the answer stared back at me from the screen of my laptop. It was admittedly unconventional, but deep down, it bore witness to my spirit as I sensed the peace of the Holy Spirit inside of me.

Right before sending the letter out, I contended with uncertainty. The Holy Spirit reminded me of all of the prophetic markers that had happened throughout the course of events leading up to the moment I would place the letter in that blue mailbox outside of my local post office.

The post office box number matched the year of his birth. I never chose the post office box number. I let the person at the post office who was assisting me pick the box number instead.

When asked by the post office employee if I wanted stamps, though I didn't need stamps, the Holy Spirit quickened in me to get stamps. The image on those stamps matched an animal the actor had seemingly randomly mentioned during an interview.

Then, there was the fascinating fact that in the season of my worst pain, where I was inspired to write about the Garden of Gethsemane, the actor was going through an existential dilemma.

And the show I had yet to learn about that the actor was appearing in where one of the characters not only shared my name but that character was based on an event that took place the same year as the year of my birth.

How many prophetic "coincidences" would it take to convince me that God was moving inside of a situation? Deep down, I knew that coincidence had nothing to do with this. It still remains to be seen why God was leading me down this path. But, it was something I would soon have an answer for.

I put the letter in the blue mailbox outside of my local post office. The Lord had shown me an indirect path to get the letter to the actor, and that is the path the letter would take.

While I waited for God to reveal to me why He was leading me down this path, the dreams commenced. It began with warning dreams. The warning dreams amplified the more intense things got for me in the physical realm. Finally, one night, an angel visited me while I slumbered. I didn't understand what it was I had witnessed in my dream until weeks later when the message he had given to me began to manifest in the physical realm.

I thought back on the dream the Lord had given me. I hadn't expected him to appear. I remembered being frustrated in the dream. I remembered the sky being so bright that the light was brighter than the light that emanated from the sun. I remembered knowing that I could not look upon his face as the angel approached me.

"It'll be okay. Everything will change after the next full moon."

And boy, did it change.

the commission

Two Months Later

I paused the video I was currently watching online. Tears silently fell down my cheeks. Though I wiped them away, new tears quickly replaced those I had absent-mindedly wiped away. The actor was straying away from the path of righteousness. He was embracing wicked things. Things that would not be pleasing to the Lord.

I inquired of the Lord, "Was this it? Was this the reason why You had put me on this path, Lord? Was this the reason why the letter the Holy Spirit had inspired was so different from what I had originally planned for it to be? Was it because he needed to hear a different message than the one that I wanted to give him?"

I remembered a video I had watched of him where he was talking about Jesus, and I had to rewind and watch again because I spotted a reflection of something in his eyes that had grabbed hold of my attention. The moment had broken open a deep spiritual truth that reminded me so much of what Scripture tells us about Jesus leaving the ninety-nine to go after the one lost sheep. It reminded me about how all of heaven rejoices over one who was lost being saved.

It reminded me of that because that was what I saw in his eyes as I watched this video. It was this fundamental awareness of the reality of a higher power that was so prevalently displayed in his eyes. He was so lost in thought as he spoke of the reality of Jesus that he seemed to temporarily lose awareness of his surroundings.

I could relate to that feeling quite well.

I was now faced with two realities vying for dominance; that he was straying from the path of righteousness and that the Lord had permitted me to glimpse that moment of recognition in his eyes so I could pause and learn to fully appreciate how beautiful it is to witness one who is lost become saved. I reflected on that moment and the magnitude of what it means for a person to enter into a relationship with Christ. It wasn't just eternal salvation that awaited and the magnitude of everything that meant for a person's eternity. It was the spiritual walk the person would take. It was the understanding that the more they pursued Christ, the more He would display Himself through that person.

It was understanding that when you gain a brother or sister in Christ, though there may be differences in time and distance and you could have never met the person before, you know one another better than most because you both stand on the same spiritual foundation. A foundation that cannot be shaken with a cornerstone that will never be removed.

The magnitude of meaning hit me like a ton of bricks. As I meditated on the reality of this situation, I learned to appreciate why all of heaven rejoices over one who is lost becoming saved, as it created unspeakably beautiful spiritual bonds connected by Jesus Himself. As long as Jesus was in it, it would produce life and love and fellowship that could not be duplicated in any other part of existence.

It made complete sense to me, as I watched this reality unfold on the screen of my laptop, why it is the Lord would use him to shake me awake and why it is the Lord would use me to help a brother in Christ who was straying from the path of righteousness.

I had confirmation of this as I sat with the Bible one night and asked the Holy Spirit to guide me to what it is He would have me focus on. It was my first time reading the Book of James, and I wept as I read the last passage of the Book of James titled "Bring Back the Erring One." I thanked the Lord and glorified Him for His grace and His mercy, and I held this confirming word close to my heart. I took a moment to appreciate how God orchestrated connections to serve multifaceted purposes.

Now, I sat and waited on the Lord for Him to guide me on the next steps He would have me take.

Two Weeks Later

"I would like to close out my post office box, please," I told the gentleman behind the counter. He had kindness in his eyes and was done with my request in a matter of moments. "That was faster than I expected," I smiled and commented as he handed me my receipt.

He returned my smile with one of his own. "Forgive me, miss, but may I ask you a question?" I nodded and stopped right as I was making my way to leave.

"I have a ticket to this movie event in New York City that's taking place in a couple of weeks. I just had something come up, and I found out I won't be able to go. I can't get a refund for it. Would you be interested by chance?" he gently inquired of me.

"That's so thoughtful. I am free. What movie is the event for?"

I watched him pull the ticket out from under the counter and look it over. "Um, it's that new movie with Atlas Merrick," he stated as he looked for the name of the movie on the ticket.

And to think, I'd just been a moment away from walking through that door. "Atlas," I stated.

The man with kind brown eyes looked back up at me. "Yeah. What do you say? Would you be interested in taking it? Do you watch his movies?"

I smiled a knowing smile. "I do. Yes, I would like very much to go," I replied to him. As he handed me the ticket, I thanked him for thinking of me. I asked him why he offered it to me instead of any other person who walked through the door. He said he had just had a feeling it would be something I might like, and I had been the first person all day to be so nice to him.

I was both sad and happy. I was sad because I was once again reminded of how desperately people needed restoration of righteousness in this hurting world. For someone to be so generous to me simply because I had been polite was a sad reflection of the current state of our society. I was happy, too, though. It brought me a joy I couldn't adequately articulate to know that the Lord was still working inside of the situation that had so impacted me.

That night I dreamt of exactly what I would wear to the event. I dreamt of each step I would take as I boarded the train that would take me into the heart of New York City. Each step that would lead me to the exact spot where the event would take place. I dreamt of a blue-eyed security guard who would help me find my seat. I dreamt of each moment with such detail it felt like I was already living it. In the dream, I could feel the air and the heat. I could feel the ticket as I held it in my hand. I could hear the noise of the city with much more clarity than one typically did in a dream.

I dreamt of each movement right up to the point where Atlas' eyes would find mine, and a look of recognition would come alive inside of his brown eyes. I watched him step forward and the dream dissipated.

Event Night

I should probably be nervous, but I wasn't. I was too focused on the subtleties of everything around me to be too caught up in nervous tension. The decision to embark on this little journey was not an impulsive one. Instead, it came into my awareness, and my spirit immediately identified it for what it was: guidance. I didn't have to question it because I knew I was being led in this direction.

So, I acted in obedience to the directive I was given.

The train pushed me, gently swaying me left and right, and I let myself be swayed by its bumpy rhythm as I pondered what would happen. Some of the things would be familiar to me, at least as familiar as a flat-screen could make it out to be. Many things I was sure would be vastly unfamiliar to me.

I looked down at my hands as they remained folded on my lap.

I knew I needed to be led in this and not let my thoughts fly away with me. I was calm and at peace with this, which was further confirmation that I was indeed being led in this. If this had truly been my decision, I would be a nervous wreck by now.

Instead of being nervous, peace filled me.

I had no idea what the next step would be outside of my showing up there. But I implicitly trusted the Holy Spirit guiding me. No matter what, this would serve a greater purpose than serving me.

Maybe he needed me.

The movement of the train jolted me out of my thoughts, and I took the opportunity to look out of the window at the sun settling along the beautiful

Connecticut shoreline. I enjoyed this peace. I was not looking forward to the chaos of the city, but I knew that's where I needed to be. I knew this was where God wanted me to be.

I closed my eyes and soaked in the golden rays of the late spring sun. I smiled at it. I took a deep breath and began to mentally prepare myself for the next steps.

No one accompanied me on this trip. I was alone, but I knew I was not meant to have company with me in this. Heading into New York City in such a circumstance was not something one would likely refer to as wise, but I knew better. No matter what the outcome was, the will of the Holy Spirit guiding me was more important than getting lost in a plethora of potential outcomes.

I looked in my purse to find my ticket.

Even the circumstances under which I had come into ownership of the ticket were far from normal. I ran my thumb over the name of the event, written in a shimmering gold color. Would anyone believe me if I told them how unusual the path was that the Lord was leading me down?

There it was. New York City. I had a funny feeling beginning to form within me. It was an expectancy of sorts. I knew I could not move until directed to do so by the Lord, but I also knew that when that feeling began, I needed to be tuned into it.

I unzipped the hidden pocket sewn into the space next to my hip. I took out my phone to check the time. The train was scheduled to arrive in the city in thirty minutes. The event was set to take place two hours from now. I would have enough time to walk there and get situated in the space set aside for onlookers.

I put my phone back in the side of my pants and zipped the hidden pocket.

It was not wise to carry a purse on me. Under normal circumstances, it would be risky enough for me to travel alone. I closed my eyes and tried to focus my mind. I waited and waited until the stirring within me began. I opened my eyes to look at that golden sun suspended above the ocean. I took in a deep breath. I was on the right path.

This was a one-in-a-million shot.

It remained to be seen what would come of my adventure, but I trusted the Lord's guidance. Lost in my thoughts as I was, I failed to recognize when the train entered the city. I failed to notice when the pace of the train began to slow. I failed to notice when it stopped altogether.

"Miss?" I came out of my mental reprieve to find a younger gentleman looking down at me. "Miss, we've arrived."

I stared at him blankly for a moment before I forced myself to move. I stood up and gave him a polite smile. "Thank you," I replied softly.

"Are you alone, miss?" I could see the glimmer of concern shining in his hazel eyes.

"I am indeed," I replied. The look in his eyes reflected his hesitancy. I gently inquired of him. "Is there something on your mind, sir?" I assessed his disposition closely and the look of fear he had that shone back at me from his kind eyes.

"I'm... I'm sorry, miss. I'm a little concerned for your safety."

I smiled up at him. "I appreciate your concern. And I appreciate you sharing it with me. May I ask you a question? Forgive me, what is your name?"

"Seth. Yes, you can ask me a question."

I smiled kindly at the young man. "Do you believe in God?" Seth nodded at me. He seemed a little surprised by my ease with asking that question. I kept smiling. "And do you believe in Jesus Christ?"

All at once, I saw the concern leave his eyes as joy lit up his hazel eyes in such a way that it made the flecks of gold in them sparkle brighter. "Yes, ma'am, I do."

"Good then. I do believe I am on a bit of an assignment. Your concern for my safety is warranted. However, I am certain you know as well as I do that the best thing to do to address such a thing is to pray for me. Will you do that for me, Seth?"

Seth nodded and swallowed noticeably. I knew how difficult it was to surrender control to the will of a higher power. The response of the flesh was one that was difficult to contend with. It was a daily struggle that seemed to manifest in different forms. One day a person could seemingly master the response of the flesh in one way, and another day, a person could contend with the response of the flesh in an entirely different and new form.

Surrendering control when the fear of the unknown caused a person to want to take control was a very difficult thing to contend with. Sometimes, a person loses the battle and surrenders to the temptation and misguidance of thinking they could do something better than the will of the Lord. Sometimes, a person wins the battle and accomplishes resisting the temptation, and the will of the Lord plays out as it was intended to play out. Those are remarkable moments when the Spirit of the Lord showed up in ways that no human mind could ever predict.

God was unexpected like that. It was always a beautiful thing to behold. The real question in such transitional moments was, could mankind step out of its own way long enough to watch God do what only God can do?

Sometimes.

But, I often wondered how many opportunities were missed, how many beautiful things were never born, because the temptation of the flesh deceived us into thinking we could somehow do it better than the Creator. So many think that they have answers to things that they could not possibly have answers for. How could an unveiled night sky be explained other than what God has said is true?

I found myself walking the streets of New York City in an automatic way. I knew where I was going, but I was not familiar enough with the layout of the city to know with such confidence where I was going without paying close attention. Only the guidance of the Holy Spirit could establish this kind of confidence I walked with.

While I was lost in the inner musings of my thoughts, I came to awareness long enough to see that I was indeed going in the direction my dream had shown me. Nervous energy flooded me all at once, and I paused in my steps long enough to re-center myself. Fear had no place in this. It was natural that I would contend with such a thing, given what I was here for.

I prayed.

I prayed and focused my mind on what had initiated my first steps in this direction, to begin with. Something deep inside of me filled me with a sense of knowing. I focused on the feeling of knowing as the awareness that this actor needed me resolved itself inside of my spirit.

I remembered watching a video of him from years ago. I remembered seeing the battle take place in his eyes. I couldn't understand why the person who was interviewing him at the time continued to ask questions. Had it been me sitting down across from him, witnessing that pain so evident in his eyes, I would have been unable to continue with my questions.

I looked down at my attire and my bare arms. I had not sought out the pure white pants and pure white corset. I had seen both while doing another task, and I had a knowing in my spirit that both were what I would wear on my journey here. When this day had finally arrived, and I looked in the mirror before making my departure, I understood why it was this. I had an ethereal look. I immediately looked away from the mirror and battled with feeling unworthy.

The Lord knew what was in my heart regarding attention. I preferred being overlooked, being unseen, being easily forgotten. But obedience to the Lord was more important to me than what I thought or felt about myself. If this was His instruction, which I was sure that it was, then I would seek to obey Him every step of the way.

I paused and looked up at the structures that made up Times Square. I was not partial to the spirit of this place, but I was focused on my assignment. I watched as the lights in the surrounding buildings began to pop on in sync with one another.

It was almost time.

My insides began to respond in a way that made my midsection feel sensitive and tender. I fought to rid myself of the sensation of tenderness but could not center my mind enough to accomplish my goal. There were too many distractions causing me to be unable to focus my mind as I needed to in this moment.

There was a reason why I did not venture into cities. The intensity of all of the activity was not something I was skilled at engaging. Without God, the hustle and bustle made me nervous and unfocused.

I took a deep breath and prayed for God to settle the storm that was quickly taking shape inside of me. He knew I didn't like the intensity of cities. Deep down, I knew this was not just about what the Lord had shown me inside of his eyes as I watched that interview; it was also about helping me step out in faith and allowing the Lord to help me grow in ways I could not grow in without Him. I took another deep breath and meditated on the Lord.

The Lord is my shepherd, I shall not want.
The Lord is my shepherd, I shall not want.
He maketh me to lie down in green pastures.
He leadeth me beside still waters.
He restores my soul.
Restore my soul Lord.
Restore my soul Lord.
Restore my soul Lord.

I did not like anything about this place. It unsettled my spirit to be here. Being here at night would only increase the unsettled feeling that was sprouting to life inside of me.

I resumed my walk to my destination.

There was too much activity as the site of the movie premiere came into view. People were beginning to crowd together, and the energy in the air was tangible. I watched the exuberance light the eyes of women and men alike as they were all being ushered into the area where the stars of the movie would soon arrive.

Stars.

I never understood why they were called by that title. Did they shine any brighter than a person like Seth? No, I daresay that, in most cases, it had nothing to do with the character of the movie star in question. The whole concept of stardom seemed like an artificial construct that separated people into classes. I wondered if all of the attention ever made those movie stars feel lonely.

While so many people got caught up in the fandom of these things, I found myself more concentrated on the true character of the person playing a character on a big screen. I wanted to know who they were. I often found myself more interested in the interviews and what kind of insight, if any, could be gained in observing the movie star in those inquisitive moments.

I watched the responses of the quickly growing crowd as the time neared. I didn't want to approach yet. Everyone was lit up with joy and expectation. Phones were in the hands of countless people, and I briefly found myself wondering how much time was occupied on those rectangular screens.

I closed my eyes and saw him in my mind's eye. The memory of the dream surfaced, and I replayed its contents for a brief moment before I prepared to immerse myself in the rapidly growing crowd. I remembered his brown eyes staring back at me with a look of surprise intermingled with expectation.

At the time I had dreamt the dream, I had no idea what it meant. I just knew that it would be soon, very soon, in fact.

Atlas.

His name whispered through my thoughts, and it felt like my spirit longed to be free of my body in that moment. What was this exactly? I knew it remained to be seen, but I found myself contending with the temptation to walk away and not see this through. I forced myself to walk toward the spot I knew I would be standing in when the dream manifested and ignore the temptation to walk away and not see this through.

I approached the entrance and the person who was clearly hired for security. I could not see his eyes through his dark sunglasses and knew it was a tactic intended to intimidate someone who may have nefarious intentions. It certainly wasn't meant to block out the sun, which was nearly absent from the skyline at this point.

I addressed one of the people who seemed likely to be on the security team. "I believe you will be requiring a ticket for entrance?"

He had been getting ready to move and speak to me as I approached, but I chose to speak first. He nodded at me. "You believe correctly, miss."

I smiled warmly at him. "May I retrieve it from my pocket?" I inherently knew it was not wisdom to go reaching into hidden places when interacting with those hired for protection purposes.

"Yes, ma'am," he replied.

His deep voice reverberated in the air around us, and I found myself temporarily distracted by thoughts of how that sound impacted the air around us. The next moment I reached into my zippered pocket and took out my pass for the event. I handed it to him. "VIP, okay. Wait one moment, please, ma'am." He dialed a number on his phone. "Hey. VIP pass holder. Okay. See you in a minute." He ended his call. "Please step off to the side here. We will have someone escort you to the front in a moment," he said.

I proceeded to do as he instructed. I watched as others were ushered into the stands. I liked that they did this. It gave people in the back a better opportunity to see what they had come here to see.

I caught sight of a tall gentleman approaching and had an odd feeling pass through me. I wanted to take time to analyze it, but there was only time to feel it, commit it to my memory, and set an internal reminder for myself to revisit it when I was afforded more time to do so.

He stopped in front of me, and I met his vivid blue eyes. "Are you the VIP?"

I handed him my pass. "That's what the pass says," I replied.

His eyes assessed me for a moment like he was trying to understand why I had chosen to respond in such a way. He looked at the pass and nodded, and handed it back to me. Though I knew my interaction with this in-dividual was likely to be short-lived, there was a part of me that knew I needed to know his name. "Forgive me, sir, but may I ask your name, please?"

He paused long enough for me to quickly assess how immaculate his dress was. His all-black suit and tie were pressed to perfection. Not a wrinkle was evident in the pristine fabric. The suit fit his large frame as though it had been tailor-made to fit him specifically. There were highlights of blond in his sandy brown hair. Though it was short and well-trimmed on the sides, I could see that evidence of blond in the strands he kept longer on top.

"Chase. I am security detail for Mr. Merrick." I felt a quickening inside of me. Now, I knew why that feeling had passed over me when I had seen him approaching me. "Come with me," he instructed.

I began to walk beside him as he led me toward the entrance. "Forgive me. Might I ask why you are not with Mr. Merrick if you are his security detail?"

Chase looked at me briefly as he led me through the hustle and bustle of the activity building on the red carpet entrance. "There are more on his detail than just me. Some are with him, and some will be at other spots to make sure there are no disruptions during the whole red carpet event."

I nodded as we continued.

He put his hand on the small of my back as he led me through the crowd at the front. There were cushioned seats set up in a balcony style, and evidently, mine was somewhere in the middle of all that congestion. Chase waited for me to settle in. "Thank you, sir," I said to him. He nodded and assessed me for a moment.

"I will come and find you after everyone walks in," he finally replied.

I looked at him, allowing him to see my confusion as I held his gaze. "I don't understand, sir."

He pointed to my ticket, which I held in my hand. "Your ticket is for entrance to the movie, not just the event leading up to it," he said.

He smiled and walked away.

That was a detail that had escaped me. Details did not typically escape my attention. I looked at my pass. There were no immediate indications to me that this was a pass for entrance into the movie as well. I mentally changed my plans. I had been prepared to leave once the events of the dream transpired and get on the train to go back home. Given this unexpected development, I now believed there was more that the Lord wanted me to discover. This wasn't just about a passing moment of visual awareness.

There was more.

What would you have me do, Lord?

Screams from the entrance caught my attention, and I gasped at the sudden burst of excitement. I sat down as people around me rushed to their seats and stayed standing up so they could catch sight of the ensuing events. I closed my eyes and tried to block out all the noise and excitement. I started hearing snippets of people speaking the names of the stars of the movie. I kept my eyes closed and tried to focus on what I needed to do.

I didn't want to stand up. I didn't want to do what the dream had shown me I would do. I sat there battling the fear of the moment, knowing full well that there was nothing about this event that I currently found myself in that spoke to the kind of person I was. I didn't want this. I had to remind myself that this wasn't about what I wanted. This was about obedience to the Lord and what He would have transpire.

I opened my eyes as I felt a flood of peace fill me.

I stood up, already knowing what would take place next. The noise of the crowd faded out as I caught sight of Atlas walking down the red carpet. Flashes from cameras and cell phones lit up the air within my sight. He was smiling and talking to interviewers as he made his way down the red carpet. He would stop on occasion and sign some pictures and items for fans. He took a few pictures as he went along.

His dark blue suit somehow amplified the dark brown strands of his stylishly done hair. A sharp pin pierced one color of his pure white dress shirt under his suit jacket. I had seen him wear a similar look in the past. I found myself partial to this look. Perhaps, it was simply because everything about this moment was true to what the Lord had shown me in the dream.

He finally made his approach toward my section. There were no butterflies or errant responses from my flesh. There was just a single-minded focus on what would happen. I focused on every detail of every movement. I watched him smile. I watched how seasoned he was with every part of these types of events. He moved along with ease and knew how to handle himself inside the hustle and bustle of such a small space with so much activity taking place.

I watched him. Every part of myself left me, and I found myself observing him with a sense of wonder and contentment. I watched the way he tucked his hands in his pockets and obliged the onlookers wanting to get a word or a moment with him.

I let my lips part so I could catch the cooling sensation of a breath passing through my parted lips. The delicate fur at the top of my corset bustled in a gentle breeze that had just picked up, and I knew. The moment was here.

Atlas looked up and directly at me. His easy smile faded as curiosity saturated his eyes.

He paused.

His eyes remained on mine in a moment of suspended time as he looked at me like he knew me. This was impossible by any standard that was measured as normal. I could see the reflection of camera lights flashing against his brown eyes. I felt a rush of adrenaline hit my bloodstream and lace itself through every part of me it could touch. I took a deep breath in an effort to try to calm myself. My nerves were suddenly on edge as his eyes remained locked on mine.

My dream had shown me everything up until the moment when Atlas took one step toward me. There were no more instructions from the Lord in the dream He had given me, so when Atlas took that step, my eyes fell to catch the movement and returned to his long enough to see someone approach him and direct him to the doors he needed to go through.

He had to look away, but before he entered the doors, he looked back to find my eyes one more time before he was forced to go through them.

the encounter

Atlas

It was her. How?

Too many questions saturated my mind in a moment when I needed to focus on my approach to the public. I needed to have complete awareness of my surroundings. I needed to be ready to pivot as needed. I needed to meet the demands that naturally accompanied events such as this one.

But all that occupied my thoughts was her.

I had dreamt of her so often that I had begun to think that I was slowly and steadily going mad. It was like a slow torture of the soul, seeing someone I had never met showing up repeatedly in dreams. It was like the death of the spirit, never being able to know her in reality. There were only those whispered, intangible, mysterious dreams to beckon me with the illusion of her existence.

Until now.

She was real.

My heart was responding to her existence. The pace of my breath was responding to her existence. My blood was responding to her existence. I found this to be the very last place I wanted to be in this moment.

What a dramatic turn of events.

I had come here expecting business as usual and got my world thrown upside down. I longed to go to her and discover who she was. But I was lost in a daze of introductions, re-introductions, and handshakes with friends I had not seen in some time. My name sounded repeatedly, but it all seemed muffled, and everything seemed to be lost in a haze of activity that paled in comparison to what had shaken my world before entering the building.

The look in her eyes.

She looked into me like she fully knew me and understood me. Her pale face was soft with the overflow of wonder and kindness that radiated from the depths of her dark blue eyes. The red tint to her short blond hair caught the last rays of the setting sun as the fur that lined the top of her corset caught the gentle breeze that had picked up.

While the crowd was busy being distracted and nearly every person held up a phone trying to get the pictures they so desired, she simply stood there uninterested in anything except looking so thoroughly at me. She held no phone. She had no companion she whispered things to, and she was clearly uninterested in shouting as many others in the crowd were doing.

She stood staring at me, lips gently parted, and tilted her head delicately to one side as she continued to let me see her.

I'd taken one step forward without thinking of the consequences of what the action would mean. My agent had certainly been thinking and swiftly steered me away from her. Every part of me had wanted to resist, but I knew it would not work.

How was I to find her now?

She had been in the front, which meant she had to have a VIP pass. What kind, though? Surely she would have needed an escort to that section. I briefly wondered if someone on my team had assisted her.

I found a quiet corner and pulled my phone out. I sent a group text to my security team.

> ME: *Did anyone happen to escort a VIP guest dressed in all white?*

I received many responses replying no to my question and found myself ready to reach out to other security teams when the last person on my team sent through his response.

> CHASE: *I did. I'm bringing her in right now. She has a premiere pass.*

My heart sped away at the thought, and I knew her seat would be in the balcony section of the theater. The bottom was reserved for the production crew, actors, and any guests they wished to invite. I couldn't go up to the balcony section. I found myself wondering how she had gotten such a pass.

Who was she?

For a moment, I thought about the possibility of asking Chase to bring her to me so she could sit in my section of the viewing area. As much as I wanted that, I couldn't have her come and sit in the bottom section with me. Maybe after the movie, I could get a moment with her during the meet and greet. That was assuming she would stay for that, though. Would she stay for that? She seemed so different from all the other pass-holders as I watched their faces light up as they found their seats on the balcony. So many of them were star-struck and caught up in the glamour of it all.

My eyes were glued to the entrance of the balcony waiting for Chase to escort her through the thick red curtains.

She didn't look around when she came through. She watched Chase lead her down to the front row of seats and turned her face up to smile warmly at him. Chase wasn't usually very receptive to people, but I watched his eyes shift down to the floor beneath their feet, give a hesitant smile that almost looked bashful, and turn back to her before he made his full exit.

That was very much unlike him.

ME: *Is she staying for the meet and greet?*

I saw a bubble with ellipses as I waited for him to respond.

CHASE: *She didn't say she wasn't when I told her I'd be back for her after the premiere. If anything, she seemed a little... like she wasn't expecting for there to even be a meet and greet.*

Was she expecting a meet and greet?

I looked up at the balcony as the lights were being lowered. She was standing at the edge staring down at me, lips parted, with a look of wonder on her face. It was a different look than the knowing look she gave me when we were outside. Her lips moved in the shape of my name, and I watched the knowing look return to her eyes.

"Atlas!"

The director's loud proclamation of my name drew my attention. I needed to take my seat and get settled in for a few hours. How was I going to do that with her nearby? I had no choice. I took my seat as the lights turned all the way down, and I settled in as the show began.

My mind drifted to her presence in my dreams. I had only ever seen her face and that look in her eyes. I had never seen more than that. But, the dreams had always felt like they went on for hours of just her face and her eyes and everything that was behind their dark blue veil.

I inherently knew the meet and greet was not going to afford me enough time with her.

ME: *Chase, get her number after the film is conclud-*
ed. If she inquires as to why, just tell her it is normal
practice.

CHASE: *Will do.*

This was the first time I was seeing the completed version of the movie, and I had been excited to see how it came out, but now I was entirely distracted. When I closed my eyes, all I saw were her eyes. When my eyes were open, all I saw were flashes of her.

By the time the movie concluded, I felt like it had been too long, but not long enough. We all talked for a bit while the balcony was cleared out from the onlookers. I hadn't gotten up in time to see her before she departed from the balcony, a fact that I was currently reprimanding myself for. I was becoming increasingly agitated and knew I needed to make progress in this, or it would continue to drive me to distraction.

ME: *Any update, Chase?*

I stared at the ellipses bubble.

I hated those ellipses bubbles in this moment but continued to watch them as they bounced across my text screen.

CHASE: *Got it. But she seems a bit reluctant to meet you, I think.*

ME: *What do you mean?*

For a woman to look at me the way she did, I would not have thought she would be reluctant to meet me. She seemed entirely too inquisitive. Entirely too open to me as I looked at her.

> CHASE: *She seems surprised by all of this. Not something I would expect from our usual VIP pass holders. When I mentioned how we were on our way to the meet and greet, she started getting fidgety and asking a lot of questions about what would happen.*

How did she get a pass like that without awareness of what it would give her access to?

My agent led me to the private area of the building, and the actors and crew members got situated and ready to meet the pass holders that had been in attendance on the balcony. Media members began to filter into the room. There were so many people. Cameras flashed, and questions began, but all I could focus on was the fact that I had not seen her come in yet.

> ME: *Where is she?*

"..."

I sighed as I stared at those ellipses.

> CHASE: *She said she needed a minute and something about how she thought she'd be on a train home by now.*

ME: *Bring her in. We're getting ready to do the meet and greets. She'll probably be last, so it will give her time to see what happens before she gets to the front.*

CHASE: *You got it.*

The meet and greets were normally a fun experience for me. I enjoyed getting to see the excitement in the eyes of the fans. I enjoyed hearing their feedback. I enjoyed the love and the adoration. I spent much of my time feeling as though I didn't deserve that adoration. I found peace knowing I brought some joy into the lives of others. This world was too harsh, and it was getting to be even harsher with each passing day.

The crowd began to thin and wind down, and it wasn't until nearly everyone had cleared out that I finally caught sight of her. Chase stood beside her. That wasn't the protocol, so she must have requested he stay with her.

I sat at the table while the rest of the crew got ready to depart. The man directing the crowd had come up to us when he saw she was the last one and said she was here to see me, so everyone else began to take their leave.

She was suddenly standing before me. It was quiet. Our only company was my remaining security team. I had excused the gentleman who had overseen leading the crowd to the person they were here to see.

She didn't seem nervous. Her gaze was direct as she stood several feet away from the table where I sat. I gripped my pen in my hand as she looked into me as she had when we were outside. I leaned forward in a motion to convey I was ready to fully engage her in whatever direction she took this.

Her eyes dropped to the pin in my collar, and I watched her smile. There was a joy that lit her eyes that I was not expecting to see. "The dark blue suits you," she said softly.

"Not a fan of the red?" I immediately knew what her comment was in reference to. No one else had made the connection. Not even the style icons who had been here before the show.

Her eyes met mine. "Fan? I've always found the concept of a fan an interesting one," she said.

The mystery of who she was started to develop into something more than I originally anticipated. "Are you not a fan?"

Her eyes remained on mine in a thoughtful way. "I don't think that word would accurately describe the way I view things," she answered.

"If you're not a fan, what brings you to this event?"

She smiled down at the floor in front of us. "That's a long story Atlas," she answered me in a soft voice.

"So, we can establish that you know me," I commented.

Her eyes came back up to meet mine and the mirth was gone. It was replaced by a rather intense expression. "We can indeed. You... you look at me as though you know me as well. Though I am certain you and I have never crossed paths," she finished.

I was so unaccustomed to her calm disposition. These events were never calm. They were always bursting with tension and nervous, excited energy. I found her calm disposition quite welcomed but highly unusual. "Can you step closer, please? It is difficult to see you with the stage lights behind you," I asked.

She waited a moment before she complied with my request. When she came a few steps closer, she looked nearly angelic. The spotlight became her halo and illuminated and intensified her already intense gaze. There was still no nervous energy I could detect from her.

"Boss, we have to clear out," Chase said.

"I know," I responded without removing my eyes from hers. The look she gave me was one I had never encountered before. It wasn't just that she looked at me as though she knew me; it was that it felt like she did know me.

"I should probably go," she said softly as she looked down at where her hands were folded in front of her.

"There are no more trains out of the city this late at night. Do you have a place you are staying?"

She didn't look up at me despite my question to her. She shook her head. "I'm sure I can find a hotel," she said as she looked up at me with a kind smile lighting her face up further. She was beginning to look ethereal.

I stood up and rounded the table. I approached her slowly, so she would have plenty of time to understand that I was approaching her. I knew the city well enough to know that she would not be able to find a hotel close by that had any vacancies. But the real reason I did what I did next was that the most dominant thing in me at the present moment was the knowledge that I could not let her go so soon. There was too much more for me to discover.

"Allow me to help," I said as I stopped a foot away from her. The scent of lilacs slowly wrapped itself around me.

"Boss, no vacancies this late at night," Chase said. She looked at Chase briefly as surprise bloomed on her delicate features.

"Oh. That presents a problem, I suppose," she said absentmindedly. "Atlas, I see how it pains you to answer questions about your mother. Why is it you do not request that no questions about her be asked of you?"

Her eyes were full of wonder and innocence that took my curiosity about her and morphed it into astonishment of her. There was no fear in her eyes about what my response would be. There was a simple innocence and compassion that robbed me of my breath. I was so overcome by her purity of heart that I failed to notice when a stray tear fell to my cheek. She watched it fall and slowly reached up to place her hand against my cheek and wipe away the evidence of the emotions that had overcome me.

She had no concern for herself. Her only concern was for my emotional well-being.

She smiled at me with compassion and took her hand away. She looked down at her hand and the moisture on her palm. She traced it with a finger of her other hand. "Tears are precious. Yet, all too often, people miss their beauty and just how priceless they are. They are looked at without empathy or viewed as displays of weakness. But the reality is that tears may just be the greatest display of strength a person can exhibit," she finished softly. I was transfixed by her. She looked up at me. "Thank you for sharing yours with me."

I observed the sincerity in her eyes as she expressed her thoughts to me. I was having trouble understanding how she knew she had no place to stay, and despite that knowledge, the thing that dominated her attention was my situation regarding questions people had about the passing of my mother. It had been too long since I had seen such compassion.

"I... I let them ask because I hope someone can draw something good from what I had with her. It pains me, but she was light and love and all things good. Can the world not afford to gain something good right now? You... are the first person to ask me something like that or observe the pain it causes me to talk about her."

"The world could indeed afford to gain some good right now," she agreed. She reached out and placed her hand above my rapidly beating heart. "Thank you for sharing her too." She removed her hand just as I was about to cover it with my own. "I should go now."

I couldn't let her leave. I needed more time with her than just a few minutes. I needed to discover how it was that I had seen her in my dreams. It wouldn't be safe for her to be in the city by herself at night. Perhaps, I could lend her a little compassion of my own.

"I have an apartment nearby. You're welcome to stay with me. As long as you promise not to tell anyone where I live, that is."

Her eyes went wide, and the rapid pace of her breath made her chest rise and fall with uneven breaths. "That is kind of you, but I cannot accept." She moved a couple of steps back, and I followed. I should have given her the space she sought. If I had, I was certain she would not have run.

But she did run.

Gone just like that, leaving behind just the memory of her image as she had been while standing before me.

"Chase," I spoke his name in a rush.

"On it, sir."

I watched Chase run after her. He would find her. He would keep his eye on her. He would bring her back to me.

I let the rest of my security team clear the area so I could leave. The trip to my apartment was heavy, with a thick cloud of loneliness. How could I miss a person who I barely knew? I didn't know the answer to that question because, in some ways, it was an entirely unfit question to ask myself. Maybe it seemed like I didn't know her because of how short a span of time we had spent in one another's presence, but if I was being honest with myself, it felt like every part of myself had awakened in the moment my eyes had first found her.

It felt like my soul knew her. Like my spirit knew things I had yet to wake up to the reality about. Like she was a precious secret that had lain dormant at the very core of my being and now was finally the time for that secret to be revealed.

CHASE: *You're not going to like this boss.*

ME: *What? What happened?*

CHASE: *I found her being tossed around by a group of guys. They bruised her up a bit, and she's shaken but won't let me say a cross word about them. Got a heart as sweet as an angel. Keeps telling me I should forgive them.*

My vision went blurry as I read his message too many times. How bad was she hurt? I was almost to my apartment and was already trying to determine which wall I was going to put my fist through to expel the anger I was currently feeling.

ME: *Bring her to me.*

CHASE: *Already heading your way.*

When I got to my apartment, I would focus on preparing a place for her to stay where she would feel safe. How bad was it? How shaken was she? How many bruises? Was there blood?

I hated not knowing. Not knowing was so much worse than I had expected it to be. What would my mom do? I felt a tear fall as I thought about her. She'd draw the angel a bath as warm as she liked, with bath salts and bubbles and candles and soft music to relax her. She'd patiently wait for her to finish and would have the fore-thought to make sure the softest robe hung waiting for her on the hook on the door. She'd set out rose oil for her skin to help it mend.

I knew what I needed to do.

"I need to make a stop before we head back to the apartment," I instructed the person driving.

"Sure, where to?"

"Any specialty spa place that may still be open," I replied.

"I know just the place."

Twenty minutes later, I was in my apartment doing exactly what I knew my mom would have done for a broken and bruised angel.

the unexpected

Aria

How was Chase here with me?

The men who had accosted me had not frightened me. I had come to the city knowing full well that there could be consequences. I had already mentally prepared myself for those consequences should I face them.

I had not been prepared for Chase or his reaction to finding the group of men knocking me to the ground and making fun of the dirt that now stained my pure white attire. I had not been prepared for Chase's expertise in handling the group of men who were taking turns hitting me and pushing me to the ground. Chase handled them as though they were nothing more than people standing in his way.

He picked me up into his arms with ease and carried me away from the dark alley that now only held those men and their groans of pain. I turned my face into the warmth of his chest. "Come along now. This is no place for an angel," he said to me. His warmth drew me closer to him.

"I am no angel," I replied.

We reached a black car with tinted windows. "Whatever you say, angel." He opened the door and settled me in before climbing in next to me. He nodded at the driver and took his phone out to text someone. When he was finished, he put his phone back in the pocket of his jacket.

"Let me have a look at you," he said as his blue eyes met mine. His hands found my face and then cupped my face so he could move it around and have a better look. "I should have done to them what they did to you." He shook his head. "Are you hurt? Do you need a hospital? What kind of low-life attacks an innocent woman? Cowards," he muttered to himself.

I put my hands against his forearms. "I don't need a hospital. I just need rest. Don't get yourself riled up and concern yourself with them. The best thing that can be done is to forgive them. It doesn't justify their actions. It just sets you free from the burden of carrying them yourself."

"I'd gladly carry them for you," he whispered as some of the anger melted from his features. I could see how helpless he felt.

"But you don't need to, and forgiveness is the only thing that can give you that kind of freedom," I replied.

His phone sounded, and he pulled it out of his pocket again. He was responding to a text with what appeared to be a lengthy one of his own. When he finally put it away, his eyes found mine again. "How can you not hate them for what they just did to you?"

"Hate never does anyone any good. It just leads to more bad things. I don't want that in my heart. I choose the opposite," I answered him. One of my eyes was beginning to swell from the attack I suffered in the alley, but I attempted to meet Chase's eyes as best as I could.

He shook his head as he held my eyes for a moment before returning to the road before us. The streets were still a bit crowded despite the late hour. It was New York City, after all.

"My job is to protect people. I understand why you would not want to carry the burden of what just happened to you, but I seek justice for offenses done against the innocent." He looked back at me briefly. "It pains me when I have to walk away from people who get away without paying the price for those offenses," he said candidly.

I tried to smile past my split lip but found the pain restricted my motions. "The pursuit of justice is a noble thing, to be sure. But can we ever truly obtain justice on this side of heaven?"

For a moment, Chase's curiosity was open to me. I could see how the question had the wheels turning in his mind as he assessed the injuries on my face. Then he pressed his lips together and drew his eyebrows toward one another, and I knew I had lost that inquisitiveness to something else. He focused on the driver and the road.

It wasn't long after we endured shared silence before the driver turned left into a parking garage tucked under a huge skyscraper.

"Where are we?"

Chase was sweeping the contents of the underground parking garage as we made our way inside. "Atlas' apartment is in this building. He wanted me to bring you here," Chase answered.

I felt my eyes go as wide as they could. I wasn't expecting this change of events. I had been thinking that Chase was going to have the driver take me to a place where there would be available hotel rooms. "I can't inconvenience Atlas. I thought you were taking me to a place that would have available rooms," I said.

Chase looked at me. "There are no places in New York City that would have available rooms tonight. New York City hotels book out well in advance. Especially this time of the year. And even if there were places that had some available rooms, Atlas wanted me to bring you to him."

I waited to see if I would have a reaction to this new development, but there was no physical reaction that was yet strong enough to overshadow the pain. As the driver parked the vehicle, I briefly wondered what the Lord was up to and what He would have me do in this moment because He clearly wasn't done working inside of this situation. Chase opened the door and offered me his hand to help me out.

I had some trouble moving from the soreness that was settling into my body, but I masked the pain as best as I could. I wasn't fooling Chase, though. He eyed me as we moved through the main lobby to the place where we would check in to get cleared to go up to Atlas' place. Once in the elevator, his eyes remained on me as I attempted to keep my eyes forward.

"You're in pain," he stated in an assessing way.

I gently lifted my shoulders in a shrug and attempted a small smile at him. "It will abate," I replied to him in a tone that was intended to try to soothe him as much as possible.

He shook his head as his vivid blue eyes remained fixed on me. "The last thing I want to do is leave you," Chase said.

I was beginning to understand the situation a little bit better now. Chase was only meant to drop me off at Atlas' place. He would be leaving after he accomplished that task. I wasn't sure how I should feel about that. I was trying to seek out the Lord for guidance, but the pain was dominating my attention at the moment.

The doors of the elevator opened, and Chase led me out. I followed closely behind him, not wanting to be far away from him either. He approached a large, dark wood door that looked somewhere between dark brown and red. Everything about this place was so modern and so clean. With a building this large, it must take around-the-clock maintenance to keep it as spotless as it was.

Chase was on his phone as he stood at the door, and I looked around to take in my surroundings. I looked back at him as he stared at the screen of his cell phone. "I don't want you to go," I stated in a matter-of-fact sort of way.

He looked up at me and sighed. "Atlas won't harm you," he stated.

"I know he won't harm me, but that doesn't change the fact that I don't want you to go," I replied to him.

The door opened, and Chase stood straighter as Atlas came into view. Atlas was still wearing the same clothes he had been wearing at the event.

The shock on his face as he took in my appearance had me looking down at the wooden floor just beneath his feet where he stood. The next moment, I felt his hands on my face as he assessed me. I closed my eyes as I remembered the contents of the dream the Lord had shown me. There had been nothing after that moment of awareness at the premiere event. I had no idea what I was supposed to do.

Atlas' voice spilled over into the silence. "Are you okay? Do you need a hospital?"

I opened my eyes to see him looking at Chase. Chase shrugged his shoulders in response.

"You look weary, Atlas," I replied to him.

He looked at me with that crossed between surprise and curiosity like he had when we had met at the question and answer session after the premiere. "I'm so sorry. You must be cold. Come in, please," Atlas said.

I felt his hand on my lower back a moment later as he gently coaxed me inside his apartment. He and Chase both followed me as I entered at Atlas' prompting. Atlas' hand dropped from me as I heard the door close behind us.

His place was quite nice. The kitchen was directly to my left, and the living space was to my right. Tall
windows made up the wall next to the living space and
had a beautiful view of Central Park. I took in a deep
breath and appreciated the peace that the view of this
little bit of nature gave me.

Directly in front of me was a hallway that led to doors.

I assessed his modern-style kitchen and the cream-col-
ored couch and chairs. It was styled so beautifully. The
table in his living space caught my attention, and though
I was keenly aware that both Atlas and Chase were watching my every move, I could not resist going over to that
table in the living space. I crouched down and ran my
hand over the edge of it. The light color and design of
the table made it look like it belonged in a beach house
in the Hamptons.

"This table is beautiful," I commented as I stood back
up and faced him.

He looked down in front of him as he smiled. "That's
my favorite piece in this whole apartment." Atlas looked
back up and at Chase. He nodded to Chase, and Chase
gave me one last look like he did not want to leave before
he made his exit.

Atlas slowly walked up to me. "I'm so sorry for what
happened to you." The sincerity in his eyes was a capti-
vating sort of thing. How many people in today's world
would let another person see something like that inside
of them? How many people would let themselves feel

something like that inside of themselves and not rush to bury the feeling?

"You didn't harm me," I stated.

I wanted to soften the concern he had for me that was so clearly displayed in his eyes and the gentle furrow of his brows. I reached up to attempt to ease his concern with a touch but became distracted by my hand and my arm. I was filthy. Dirt smudges were on my hand and up my arm.

I dropped my hand as I looked down to further assess myself.

My corset was ruined and no longer glistened in any light. My white pants were worse. Well, they had served their purpose, I supposed. I remembered Atlas touching my back to guide me in as I entered his apartment. "I didn't get dirt on you, did I?" I assessed him as he shook his head to answer me with a "no," and I saw a sheen of tears in his eyes.

"Why are you sad?"

His tears captivated my attention. "Come with me," he stated as he walked past me toward the hall. He turned back to me when I made no motion to do as he had instructed me. The look in his eyes stole my breath from me. There were no words that could be exchanged between us in that moment that would have more accurately described what was being communicated between him and me just then. There was sorrow mixed with curiosity and such tenderness in his gaze. It filled me with wonder.

I followed him.

He led me into a room that I suspected was his. We walked past elegant furnishings and through another door. He let me enter first.

A stand-alone porcelain bathtub sat in the center of the bathroom. There was a very modern-style standing shower in the corner that was closed in with glass. The bathtub was filled with bubbles. Candles were everywhere. Rose petals were scattered about. A wooden bench was built in against the wall to the left of where we stood. There was an assortment of what looked like oils and lotions there. A change of clothes was set there as well as a pure white robe.

I wanted to walk out so I wouldn't get this immaculate presentation dirty.

I felt his eyes on me as he stood to my right.

"I hope you don't mind, but when Chase told me what happened, I wanted to...."

I turned to meet his gaze when he left his sentence unfinished.

"Care for you," he finally said.

I let myself assess his features as I was entirely transfixed by the way he held himself and the emotion that he kept in check. I was curious why he chose to let me see the emotions that he was currently letting me see.

He gave me a tight smile and turned to leave. "There is a lock on the door if that would make you feel more comfortable. Take all the time you need."

"Atlas, wait," I rushed my words out just as he was making his exit through the door. "I am grateful. I am grateful to you for this kindness," I said.

He gave me a tight smile and pressed his lips together. Without another word, Atlas left. I heard the soft click of the door closing behind him and took a moment to try to understand the enigma that he was.

He didn't even know my name, and yet he had clearly gone out of his way to give me this scene before me to attempt to comfort me in my pain. The fact that he had even sent Chase after me was highly unusual for someone in a position like him. He needed security to help him get from point A to point B without any incidents occurring, and yet he went out of his way to accommodate a strange woman he had never met before. There was an awareness in his eyes that made me think I may not be as much of a stranger to him as it seemed to me like I was. That awareness I saw reflected in his eyes made me so very curious.

My body took that moment to grab my attention. The pain was more than I was letting Chase or Atlas be made aware of, but I could manage it well enough. My curiosity about Atlas would have to wait a moment. I needed to clean the reminder of the assault I had suffered in the alley away from me.

I looked down at the dirt that was smudged everywhere. My arms were even coated in it. I was grateful it had dried enough on the way here that I didn't track any of it in on his floor. It would cause a mess when I discarded the clothes. I would clean it as best as I could after the bath.

A short time later, I submerged myself in the hot water of the bath Atlas had drawn for me. I wasn't one to get emotional, but in this moment, as the water cocooned me and the bubbles surrounded me, I felt exactly as Atlas had said he wanted me to feel—cared for.

the connection

Atlas

She was here. My damaged angel. Bruised, but not broken. Somber, but not in despair. Clearly weary but unwilling to move her eyes away from me. She sat there on the coach as I sat in one of the chairs positioned directly across from her. She said not one word but kept her eyes fixed on mine. Her inquisitiveness was evident in the deep ocean of her eyes. The off-white camisole and pants I had gotten for her made her look ethereal.

When I had seen the condition she was in as I had opened the door to find her and Chase waiting, I had wrestled with the warring emotions of rage and utter sadness for what she had suffered through. I wished I had never let her out of my sight. But here she was now, and I wanted to comfort her as best as I knew how to as she sat there with her hands together, placed in her lap.

"Thank you," she said in a gentle tone of voice as she was the first one to break the long silence that had suspended itself between us. The swelling on her cheek next to her eye seemed to be going down a bit. "Atlas, why am I here?" she asked.

Though her question was a straightforward one and could come off as confrontational, the tone with which she delivered her question conveyed only gentle inquisition behind the words. "I wanted you to have a safe place to stay," I responded to her. She looked down at her hands. She wouldn't look at me for quite some time as she lent time to her thoughts.

"You're not the only one I could be safe with. Why am I really here, Atlas," she finished softly as her deep blue ocean eyes found mine again.

I sighed. I supposed the only way to answer her was with the question I had been secretly asking myself. "Would you believe me if I told you I dreamt about you?"

I gave her a tense smile and tried to restrain the sudden manifestation of tears in my eyes. What else could I give her as an answer other than the truth? Could she believe me? I could barely believe it myself.

I looked up to find a small smile on her lips. Surely, it caused her pain to smile with her lip split as it was. Her smile didn't fade, though. Her eyes were alight with an internal light I didn't know how to properly describe. There was a knowing that was reflected in her eyes that had me captivated. I found I wanted to understand where that knowing was coming from.

"Indeed. I can certainly believe you," she said.

Her response was not the one that I had expected. I had expected her to laugh at me or look at me with doubt or speculation. But she was waiting patiently for me to elaborate.

"I've seen you in my dreams for some time now. So much that I thought I was going crazy. I've never met you before, so how could I dream about you and know your face with such clarity when I had never met you before," I said as a mounting tear finally fell over the rim of my eye.

She eyed me with patience and understanding as she waited for me to settle my emotions. How could I, though? This was shaking my foundation. I'd had more than enough of the foundation-shaking lately. Now, this inexplicably odd event? I didn't know how much more I could take.

"How does a universe as vast as this spin around the way it does without collapsing in on itself?" Her question stunned me into silence. My emotions settled as I tried to understand exactly who this person sitting before me was. "We see unexplainable things take place every day. Sometimes, we just forget to recognize them for what they truly are. Sometimes, we forget to dig deeper and discover more about the unseen things," she said softly.

I stood up abruptly. She didn't have anything to drink or eat, so I made my way to the kitchen to get her some water and something to snack on as I meditated on what she'd said. When I returned, I set the items before her on the table. As I leaned down, my eyes were drawn to that light that seemed to constantly radiate from her eyes. Where did something like that come from?

She didn't shy away. She held my gaze and searched my eyes clearly, trying to find something. Would I know it when she found what she was looking for?

I saw a tremble travel the length of her shoulders and realized I hadn't gotten her enough to wear to keep her warm. I immediately took off my dark blue navy blazer and proceeded to wrap it around her shoulders.

Her eyes never left mine, even as I knelt before her.

"I'm sorry I didn't think to get you more to keep you warm," I said.

"You have nothing to apologize for. You have been very gracious to me," she answered me. She had that look in her eyes still. It was like she knew me somehow, but I knew that we had never met before this day.

"I don't know how to explain how I keep seeing you in my dreams," I started. She patiently waited for me to continue. She pulled the edges of the blue blazer together as another tremble shook her shoulders. No doubt, the adrenaline that had surely hit her system during her attack was finally beginning to wane from her system.

"I also don't know how to explain how it is you have that look in your eyes like you know me," I dared submit to her for her consideration.

"That, Atlas, is a complicated answer," she said as she continued to search my eyes.

There was not one part of me that wanted to look anywhere else except at her. I wanted to know what secret she held underneath the ocean of her eyes. "We have time," I offered to her.

She pressed her lips together and winced at the pain from her split lip. Her eyes became serious as she prepared to elaborate further. I watched the intensity of whatever was taking shape inside of her grow as she looked at me. "Would you believe me if I told you God used you to draw me out of a season of deep spiritual despair?" I felt my lips part in surprise at her candor. "And that I dreamt of my trip to New York City and every step I would take that would lead me up to the moment at the premiere where you saw me and took that one step forward?"

I stood up and walked over to the floor-to-ceiling windows to look out over Central Park as the implication behind her words permeated everything around us. What she was implying was not possible. Was it? I suppose I could believe helping her out of a season of spiritual despair, as she had put it, but God actually showing her every step she would take until that moment at the event?

"I told you it was complicated. And that's not even the half of it, Atlas," she said softly. When I turned to face her, her eyes were downcast. Her hands were back in her lap as they had been before. The light was still evident in her eyes, but there was a somber air around her now, and I found I didn't like that my response was what caused that somberness to be there. I had been the one to encourage her to elaborate, and now I was reacting in a way that she had probably anticipated, given her reluctance to tell me to begin with.

She hadn't even been somber regarding her attackers. Instead, she had demonstrated to Chase all the reasons why it was so important that he let it go and not let the event or its aftermath take root inside of him. She deserved justice for what had been done to her, and yet she had focused on forgiveness.

Was my reaction to her honesty really that bad to cause her such somberness?

I reached for the only thing I could because I had no idea how to even have a conversation about her being shown things by God. "Tell me about the season of deep spiritual despair that you spoke about before," I gently coaxed her as I continued to lean up against the wooden post next to the windows. I put my hands in my pockets as I prepared to stay positioned here as she spoke.

I waited, but she didn't speak.

"Please," I whispered. Why did my chest hurt at the thought that I had caused such a change in her disposition? I tried to hold back the tears, but they seemed so easily shed around her.

She slowly looked at me. The markers of hurt were there. Her lip trembled. "It's not something I like to talk about. It's easier to talk about how God orchestrates things to work out in a way only He can. It's easier to give Him all the glory because only He can do what He does, and it is always amazing when He moves," she finished.

She must know me well enough to know that I didn't shy away from the God conversation. I was admittedly in a very shaky place in my spiritual life at the moment.

If this had been me and her four years ago, I would dive in without second thought about being cautious with the spiritual things about life. I would be hungry to know more about how it was that God had shown her the steps she would take to the moment of our interaction in that crowded place. I would want to better understand that smirk she had when I mentioned I had dreamt of her.

But it wasn't four years ago. The only thing I had in common with that man from that time was the common component of spiritual crisis. I couldn't burden her with that, though, not after what she'd suffered through tonight.

Something in me knew I could relate to her about her season of spiritual despair.

I went back to my chair to sit down across from her. I crossed my hands over my lap as I leaned back against the chair and crossed my legs. I looked at her pointedly. "I won't press you, but I would genuinely like to understand what you mean." I hoped she could see the sincerity in my eyes.

She pressed her lips together again as I watched her debate play out in her eyes. The somberness had melted away from her, and she finally sighed. "Very well," she relented.

"I thought I was losing it," she said.

"Losing what," I interrupted her.

"My salvation," she answered with the birth of tears in her eyes.

I leaned forward and propped myself up with my elbows on my knees. I didn't know what to say. I hadn't been expecting that answer from her. Something inside of me stirred to life with immediate awareness. I waited for her to continue.

"It's been difficult for me to watch it day in and day out, people in pain, suffering, and the outbursts of rage and violence. I'm not built for a world increasing in darkness. Not when I have seen the beauty of redemption firsthand."

I shook my head back and forth like I could deny what she was saying just by saying no with my motion. I watched tears fall from her eyes.

"Over and over, Atlas. I watched people fade away into the darkness, and the only way I knew how to handle it was to let myself grow numb to it. But that's not how I was built," she sniffled as she wiped the tears away from her cheeks. Those tears she wiped away were soon replaced by new ones.

"I was built for a world that demonstrates love like Christ demonstrated on the cross," she hiccupped. "You know of what it is I speak," she addressed me.

I nodded slowly and thoughtfully. I couldn't deny her that common ground with me. I wouldn't deny her that.

"I grew so numb I thought I was losing it. I stopped praying as the burden of spiritual oppression grew upon me, and I quickly became a shell of what I had once been. I stopped dreaming. There wasn't even rest for me in the spirit," she wiped at more tears as they fell.

I fought against the urge to go to her and comfort her. I wanted to comfort her, but I needed her to continue. How could I pull her out of a place like that?

When she finally settled, she looked down at where her hands rested on her lap. She smiled a small smile. "I saw your movie when it came out in November, and I couldn't figure out why there was one scene that would not leave me be. It took a few weeks for the Lord to finally shake me awake enough to see why. I saw redemption in the scene in the end. I could see the reflection of pain in your eyes, and I recognized that look. It's a look of someone who understands deep pain."

She took in a shaky breath. "I didn't follow your work much up until then. Originally, I searched other films you had done to see if I could identify the same thing I had seen in this film. The Lord quickly led me to interviews you had done instead." She paused to look at me and assess my reaction. She was timid about it.

All I could do to encourage her to continue was give her a tight smile.

"One of the first interviews I came across, you spoke about Jesus. My jaw literally dropped," she laughed as she remembered. "But it wasn't like a passing thought. You spoke about Him with passion, and I could see markers of Christ in you as you spoke about Him. After being under the barrage of witnessing darkness grow so rapidly, hearing you talk about Christ was like a healing balm to my soul. It was that little ray of sunshine I needed to see in the midst of the darkness of my night," she paused.

I shook my head like I was trying to deny her words. But how could I deny her reality? That wasn't fair of me, and I knew it. I had no right to take that from her or its impact on her. I felt the tears as they fell from my eyes.

"You are a humble man, so it does not surprise me that you would deny this," she started again. "But that doesn't change the fact that I prayed for the first time in a long time just so I could thank God for showing me the light inside of you. It was what I needed to see to save me from the suffocation of my own spiritual despair. This world has grown so dark, Atlas. It has grieved me so much to watch it happen. I tried to insert some of God into it, but they were seeds that fell on stony ground that could never take root and grow. I was too focused on fighting this battle in the flesh. It was the wrong battle strategy as this battle is spilling over from the spiritual realm."

I sat back in the chair. I didn't know what to say. What I did know was that I was intertwined with her in ways I was only beginning to understand. Deep down, I knew I was just scratching the surface of all of this.

"My dreams of you began in November," I stated.

I watched her lips part, and surprise light up her eyes.

"May I ask you a question?" she finally asked. I nodded to her. "You have seemed weary of late. Is it due to the dreams?" she finished softly.

"In part, yes. I just finished a press tour for the show I just did, so I have had months of non-stop activity. To-night's event is my last one for a bit. I'm tired in general, but the dreams have certainly exacerbated my weariness. It's been quite frustrating dreaming of only your face for so many months but never having the ability to see you until now. Why do you ask?" I replied.

She drew the edges of my blazer closer to her to lock in her own warmth. I liked that I could give her that measure of comfort. After hearing what she'd just shared with me, I had apparently given her much more than that.

"When I first started having dreams of a," she paused to assess me as she spoke, "decidedly prophetic nature, they were so vivid and so potent that I often found myself weary. It took some time and seeking the Lord's guidance for me to adjust to those types of dreams and understand them for what they were," she said.

Prophetic dreams.

I didn't know much about what she was referring to. I knew depictions of what the culture viewed as fate or destiny, but prophecy was something I considered to be in a league of its own. I eyed her as my curiosity won over my pride. "So, you were given a dream about your trip here?"

She nodded. "I knew which train I would take. I knew what time of day it would be. Without any assistance, I knew which direction to go in to find the place where the event would be. I knew Chase's face well before I ever put a name to him. I saw you stand exactly where you did and look at me exactly as you had. I saw that step you attempted to take forward," she finished softly. "And that was the last thing I was shown," she added in a whispered voice.

She looked away from me. No doubt she didn't want to see my doubt play out in my eyes. She seemed to have a higher level of emotional intuition than most people I met. I could understand how that could become a burdensome thing when presented with the emotional conflicts of others.

What was I supposed to do with all of this information? I wasn't in a place where it was easy for me to believe it all. Could I deny it? Clearly, the answer to that question was no. It had all of the markers of being orchestrated by something well beyond her and well beyond myself. I was still having trouble embracing it, though. After what I had endured with my mother and watching the world be so insistent on burning itself to the ground, it made me question everything I thought I knew.

"I watched someone ask you in an interview about your mother's passing. I remembered thinking the line of questioning was rather dispassionate. I couldn't imagine doing that without taking the empathetic approach first and foremost. But, I could never imagine putting it out there for everyone to see."

She looked back at me, and there was something in her eyes I could not quantify. It was like she could read the writing on my soul.

"There are things that happen in life that are never meant to be thrust out there for everyone to look upon. There are tragedies that bend us, break us, and shape us into something new. There are people God sends to help a person in those seasons. As she asked you those questions, I saw the look in your eyes change in a split second. I saw the pain it caused you. I remembered thinking that I couldn't do it," she said.

"Do what?" I asked her past my tears and the ball of emotion that had formed in my chest.

"I couldn't ask you questions like that, see that reflection of pain, and just continue on as though that pain did not exist. As though I did not witness it for myself. I would risk you hating me if it meant I could help you find peace inside your storm."

I tried to hold it all together, but I couldn't. I was like a dam whose structure just sustained an earthquake; I broke. I covered my face with my hands as the panic of every situation that had been weighing me down hit me all at once.

I felt her arms go around me and her sharp intake of breath as her movement caused her pain from her injuries sustained this night. I melted into her without thinking. I couldn't think as the pain was bursting forward like a tidal wave.

I couldn't outrun it.

I rested my head in the crook of her neck as she wrapped me tighter in her embrace. "I can't take it," I whispered in her ear. I let my arms wrap around her and immediately felt guilty when the pressure against her bruised ribs made her groan in pain. She held me tighter still despite the pain I had caused her.

"Not on your own, you can't," she whispered back. "The burdens of life are too great for us to bear on our own."

She let me stay there like that with her. She let me cry. She let me whisper broken sentences about how wonderful my mother was and how much I missed her. How her passing was like losing a vital part of myself. How I felt so completely, fundamentally altered, and I didn't know what to do with that feeling.

She consoled me. She whispered Scripture verses back to me to help me as I grieved. She reminded me that Jesus said His yoke was easy and His burden was light, but how we could only receive that promise when we sought Him out to comfort us in our pain. She reminded me that this is not the life, that a greater eternity awaits us that is filled with all the things God promised us. A place where there are no more sorrows, suffering, or pain. A place where there are no more tears. A place established by the omniscient God who counts every single tear we shed as precious in His sight.

I moved to the couch at some point so I could lie down. She kneeled next to me. I fell asleep there to that light in her eyes that shone down on me with compassion and kindness as she continued to whisper to me all the promises of God and how much Christ loves each one of us.

the separation

Aria

I looked down at Atlas, where he still lay sleeping. The morning sun was blooming on a new day. I knew I would soon leave him.

I had fallen asleep with my head resting on my arm next to where he lay. I had woken up very stiff, and as soon as I moved from my perch on the floor next to him, my body replied to me with a generous influx of pain. I may have to get my ribs checked when I return home.

Return home.

I didn't want to leave him. But the Lord had given me a dream last night, showing me that was precisely what I needed to do. I knew God had orchestrated this with perfect timing. It was no coincidence that Atlas was now officially taking a break, and the Lord brought me here when He did.

Atlas needed every moment of last night. He needed the reminder of the One who oversaw all of the craziness and brokenness of life. He needed that reunion.

He needed time with God. He needed time to meditate on everything. He needed space to find the healing that only God could give him.

I smiled down at Atlas. I winced as my split lip restricted my motion with pain. I would miss him, but I would forever count what the Lord had done yesterday as a precious treasure to store up in my heart.

He never mentioned the letter I sent him those many months ago. Suffice it to say he didn't know it was me who had sent it. Part of me had wanted to tell him last night, but the moment he let out his grief, I knew there was nothing more important than giving him that space to express his pain and remind him who holds all of that and what God can do inside of it.

I briefly wondered if he had ever received the letter.

It didn't matter now. All that mattered was that it was now time for me to leave. I had done as the Lord had led me to do, and I now needed to do that again.

I quickly and quietly looked for a piece of paper and a pen. I found one in the kitchen. I wrote a short note to him.

For everything you are, I thank you. Not many would have shown me the kindness you did last night. Remember, Atlas, only the love of Jesus is powerful enough to mend the deepest of wounds.

Your friend in faith.

I placed the note on the table beside him. I leaned down and gently kissed him on the forehead and prayed for his peace and for the Holy Spirit, the Comforter, to come into this place and give him the healing that only He could give.

Atlas

I woke up feeling like I had been hit by a hundred Mack Trucks at the same time. I groaned as the throbbing in my head only intensified as I sat up on the couch. I rubbed at my swollen eyes as I tried to get my bearings straight.

The events of yesterday came flooding back to me.

I opened my eyes to look for my broken angel, but she wasn't near me. I felt panic hit me but chided myself as I knew there were other places in my apartment she could be. I got up and looked around, but she was nowhere to be found.

I felt my chest tighten with real panic.

Where was she? Maybe she'd gone out for something. Maybe she was hungry or needed to get some air.

I saw a little slip of paper on the table that had not been there last night. There appeared to be writing on it. I closed my eyes and put my head in my hand. I didn't have to read it to know she was gone. Like, really gone.

I felt a hitch in my chest, and though I tried not to cry because I had done so much of that last night, I couldn't stop the tears from falling. She'd given me more than I could ever thank her for. I had so much more I wanted to know and wanted to talk to her about.

I reluctantly reached for the little slip of paper and read her note.

My eyes went wide. It couldn't be. I re-read it to make sure I was reading it right. There it was, written plainly for me to see. "Your friend in faith" stared back at me, and I couldn't believe it.

I had tried to find the person who had written me that letter. The person who had found a way to get it to me despite the fact that I had no address for fan mail to be sent to or anything like that. I remembered being impressed by the person's determination and diligence in getting something so honest to me.

I remembered reading it, re-reading it, and re-reading it.

I went to my bedroom to grab the letter from the drawer of my nightstand. I sat on my bed and read it yet again. I sighed as I finished it. Of course, it was her. It had the markers of her personality imbedded all throughout the letter. I should have known. I should have made the connection, but I was too lost in the unusual circumstances, her pain, and my grief to even consider that the same person who wrote me such an open and honest letter that impacted me much more than she knew would be the same person that had held me while I drowned within the waves of my grief.

It was her.

She was gone, and I didn't even know her name.

This was way more complicated than I originally thought it had been.

Five Weeks Later

"Hey, Aria."

I looked up from the salad I was picking at when Jackson called my name. His eyes moved from looking at something off in the distance to looking at me. I noted the look of subtle alarm in his bright blue eyes. "What is it?" That look had me a little concerned. Jackson never really got that kind of alarmed look in his eyes.

He sat back in his chair as he rubbed a hand over his short black hair. "Uh. If I remember correctly you mentioned something about writing to Atlas Merrick, yeah?" I nodded. "Yeah. It was that interview that I saw. It moved me so much that I simply had to write to him. He's so different, and I find that refreshing, I guess. I like how conscious he is of the importance of remaining humble and how... he's so contemplative," I finished.

Memories came flooding back to me as I sat there with my friend. I hadn't told anyone about my trip to New York City or what had taken place while I was there. I was surprised by the sudden rush of emotion I felt as I remembered that day. It has changed so many things about my life and my spiritual walk with the Lord. There was a part of me that longed to be able to tell him one day. I smiled as I thought to myself that I would be able to tell him one day. If not on this side of heaven, then in heaven itself.

Jackson leaned forward, and his dark eyebrows rose up. "I get it. You heart him."

I laughed. "It's not quite like that. I... I guess I appreciate his disposition. It feels rare to find it these days." I looked over Jackson's shoulder at the view of the ocean and took a moment to close my eyes and let my senses engage my surroundings.

"So, then it sounds like you'd like to meet him one day?"

For a moment, I thought that maybe I should have told Jackson, but Jackson didn't believe in God, so how would I even be able to explain the events that had transpired? I realized I had made the right decision as I thought about how much Atlas had trusted me that night as he grieved the loss of his mother. I could never breech that trust he had placed in me.

I looked back at Jackson. "Uh. I mean... I don't know. How does that even work? I'm not going to go hunt him down if that's what you mean. I've always felt that kind of thing seemed so forceful."

"I can understand that, but what if it just happened?"

"What do you mean?"

"Like... what if you just happen to run into him. Or... he happened to run into you?"

My eyes went wide. I'd finally caught on to where Jackson was going with all of this. "Is he... here?"

Jackson nodded slowly.

I froze.

All of my senses went into overdrive as I was suddenly hyperaware of my surroundings. I felt the warm ocean breeze against my bare arms. I felt the warmth of the mid-afternoon sun shining through the trees and casting some of its rays onto us. My eyes were aware of everything. The clouds off in the distance were bright white, and it almost hurt to look at them. The sunlight glittered off of the surface of the ocean. My ears were suddenly hearing everything around me, but I detected no hint of Atlas' voice.

I'd seen enough of his movies to recognize his voice were I to hear it. Those hours I had spent with him in the shelter of his apartment imbedded the sound of his voice in my soul. As my fingers pressed into the nearly white linen of my khaki capris, I knew that there would never be a day when I did not recognize his voice.

"Um. He's not just here."

I found Jackson's eyes again. "What does that mean?"

"He's looking at you."

"That doesn't mean anything," I replied. I knew that wasn't true, but I was finding it difficult to navigate a situation where Jackson did not know that I was already acquainted with Atlas. I was finding it difficult to navigate a situation in which Atlas had somehow found me after all these weeks. I hadn't expected to see him again after I had left him that morning.

"That might be true if it wasn't for the fact that he hasn't stopped looking at you," Jackson said as he smiled at me.

I felt my face flush and took a moment to wonder why it was I still had moments in my life when I reacted like this. "First thing's first, if you're lying to me, I really will be upset with you this time. Second, I need to get out of here," I finished with a sigh. I was starting to feel the pressure of the situation, and I didn't know how long I could stay in such a condition.

"Are you crazy? You heard me, right? Atlas Merrick is literally like five tables to your left staring at you, and you want to leave?"

"Jackson, you know me well enough to know that I am not a fangirl. Wait, that sounded better in my head."

"I know what you're saying. Despite your interest in his personality, you're not the kind of person to jump on the opportunity when it is in front of you. Or, in this case, to the left of you." Jackson thought about his words and seemed satisfied with the way they had come out.

"Exactly. And I am also trying to say that it is seriously freaking me out right now that he's staring at me because the only reason why someone like him would be staring at someone like me is if he somehow found out who I am. And that was not supposed to happen," I whispered in an exaggerated voice while I leaned forward as if to drive my point home.

I took a brief moment to appreciate just how true my words were. I hadn't realized that maintaining my anonymity had somehow become a security blanket for me. It protected me and gave me the ability to be the person I needed to be for him that night. It had given me courage and strength and boldness to see through what the Lord had wanted me to do.

Now, faced with the realization that Atlas being here had to mean that he somehow found out who I was, changed everything. There was so much that seemed suspended in the air between us. There was so much to explain to him, but how? Where would I even begin?

"Wait, you wrote to him using a fake name?"

"Not exactly. I wrote to him and didn't give him my name," I answered.

"But how could he tie you to this area?"

My eyes went wide as I simply shrugged my shoulders. Oh, if Jackson only knew half of the story.

Jackson held up his hands in mock surrender. "Okay. Okay. Well. In that case, your world might be about to shift on its axis."

"No. No shifting axis. Or is it axes?" I shook my head. "Either way... no." Why was I suddenly feeling panic rising within me?

"Do you seriously not feel the hole he is staring into your head right now? How are you not looking back at him?"

"Believe me... it is not without a great deal of effort on my part," I replied.

"Why are you so reluctant to interact with him? That didn't seem to bother you when you mailed your letter to him." Jackson threw a hand up and looked over at where I assumed the man of the hour was sitting.

"Don't look at him!"

Not only did he look at him. He smiled and waved.

Oh, my goodness.

This was quickly turning into the mother of all disasters. He would know we were talking about him now. And if he really was here because he somehow found out I had been the one to send him that letter, then that meant he was also now aware of the fact that I knew he was here.

"I am seriously questioning my friendship with you right now," I mumbled to Jackson.

Jackson just continued to smile at Atlas. "No, you're not. You love me," he said as he finally returned to looking at me.

"Debatable," I replied with a sigh.

I took a deep breath and prepared to do the very thing that I did not want to do. I turned to my left to find him. It wasn't difficult to spot him. He was alone and seated, so I was in his direct line of sight. All of the tables around him were empty, which I had a feeling probably had to do with the security team that was currently overseeing the entrance to this little outdoor patio. I spotted Chase and smiled as I remembered how kind he had been to me.

The look on Atlas' face was kind but serious. My breathing went all uneven on me as I thought about the words I had written in that letter. His eyes seemed to convey that he knew me better than he had after that night in his apartment, and I suppose, in some sense, he knew an aspect of me. I hadn't really been thinking about that when I wrote the letter. Honestly, I hadn't thought he would ever read it. I knew he liked to try to keep his ego in check, so the likelihood of him reading mail was slim at best. My letter hadn't been a doting kind of thing. It had been an inquisitive kind of thing. I had asked questions about things that were oftentimes overlooked, and I pondered over the deeper aspects of life and what made it beautiful. I had penned it like I was talking to a friend, hoping to find some common ground.

I gave him a confused look when his eyes remained on mine.

I was the first one to look away. I noted how the pace of my heart picked up, and I tried to settle my suddenly unsettled nerves. I had so many questions, all of which would go unanswered. I groaned. "I wish I had never written that letter," I said, putting my head in my hand for just a moment.

"That's not true," Jackson responded.

"What am I supposed to do?" I threw up my hand for emphasis.

"That's a good question, and I am not a hundred percent sure, but I do know that he hasn't looked away from you once," he replied with a sarcastic smile.

"Wonderful. That makes me feel all sorts of fantastic."

Jackson looked over at Atlas. I just kept my eyes on him and tried to ignore the overwhelming feeling of being watched. "Wow, Aria. What did you put in that letter?"

I moved my salad away. I hadn't had much of an appetite before, and I definitely didn't have one now. "Oh, you know me. You know how I get," I said in an attempt to be nonchalant.

Jackson's eyes came back to me. "You went all philosophical on him, didn't you." Jackson laughed. "I must admit, I love watching you squirm. This is actually quite entertaining. I think that I really like his shirt. Maybe I should go over and ask him where he got it."

Jackson made a move like he was going to get up. I froze him in place with an icy glare. "Do it, and I will disown you as my friend."

He shrugged his shoulders as he stayed in his seat. "It might be worth it if I get to watch how all this plays out."

We were quiet for a moment, and I tried to just focus on the sound of the waves hitting the shore or the seagulls or something. Anything. "Is he still staring?" I lowered my eyes as I waited for Jackson to give me a progress report.

"Oh yeah. He hasn't moved. So, seriously, what did you put in the letter?"

"I just talked about stuff I feel is overlooked. I talked about the deeper aspects of life, you know? I made notes of the things about life that make it truly beautiful. I mean... I just wrote it in a way where I guess it could come off like I was talking to a friend."

Jackson's eyebrows rose. "Well, that makes sense why he hunted you down. That's his wheelhouse, my friend."

Deep down, I knew it was more than that. I couldn't share that with Jackson, though. I had to respect Atlas' privacy.

"No, hunting me down is not his wheelhouse. However, this is helping me to appreciate what celebrities must go through on a constant basis. I'm not a fan of it, I must say."

"You literally hit on things that my celebrity friend over there is like constantly mindful of. I've seen some of his interviews. He literally gravitates to the deep stuff. Who's got two thumbs and loves the deep stuff?"

I pointed my thumbs at myself. "This girl," I said rather unenthusiastically.

"Exactly. Geez. He must have been super determined to find you. Even being able to narrow down your location to a place doesn't guarantee that he is going to be able to spot you," Jackson said thoughtfully. He grabbed a fry from his plate and popped it into his mouth.

"You don't say?"

He took time to eat before responding to me.

"Hey. Don't get all sassy pants on me. He's the one who's got you all in a tizzy." Jackson looked over at Atlas again and gave him a nod.

"Seriously?"

Jackson shrugged his shoulders again. "What? Look, if he is persistent about staring at you, then I'm not going to give him the cold shoulder. I'm going to be polite."

"Yes, and I am going to be over here contemplating the existential dilemma of mankind!"

"Why don't you just talk to him? He clearly came a long way to see you and figure out what is behind those big blue eyes of yours." He winked at me and grinned.

"That's not funny." He took a bite at another fry. "Even if I wanted to talk to him, which I don't."

"Liar."

"Which I don't! I have no idea where I would even begin. What? I walk up to him and say what exactly? 'Hey Atlas, uh, you might remember me from that super deep letter that I sent you several months ago. How did you find me exactly?'"

Jackson gave some thought to my words. "I'd probably lead with something else."

"Such as?"

"Hmm. 'Hi, Atlas. I'm Aria. Nice to meet you.'"

Except I had already met him. I rolled my eyes.

"You should probably, you know, look at him more than once."

I shook my head. "My world, his world... don't mix. Oil, water. Apples, oranges. Up, down."

"Night, day?" Jackson added to my analogy.

The wind started going out of my sails. "Don't you think he gets that already, though?" He asked me.

I looked down at my lap. "I... yes. I think he gets that. I think there's probably a part of him that misses the simplicity of not being known."

Jackson chuckled and drew my attention back to him. "What?"

He shook his head. "And you wonder why he hunted you down."

I shook my head. "He's an amazing actor, but he's such a profound human being, and I can't," I let my thought go unfinished as I put my hands together and moved my fingers in opposite directions like they were creating their own friction and opposition to one another. "I can't...."

"Stop. You're doing what you always do. You're anticipating a fallout before you even explore the idea of something really cool happening."

"Like what exactly?"

Jackson eyed me as silence wrapped us in its cocoon. He pointedly turned his head toward Atlas. "You need to figure out why he hunted you down."

I thought about that for a moment while I wiped my pants at something that wasn't there. "Well, technically, I made the first move, so shouldn't he kind of grab the reigns at this point?"

Jackson chuckled at me and took a sip of his water. "All right. So it's a game now, yeah? Are you keeping a tally? Okay. So, you reached out first, one point for Aria. He literally hunted you down and traveled here to find you and likely had to do some digging to find you once he got here. How many points should I give Atlas?"

"I think I deserve more than one point," I argued. If Jackson only knew the whole story.

"I'll give you five max. It does take a little courage to try."

I held up ten fingers. Jackson shook his head. "Not just because it took courage for me to do it, but because of the content that I put in it."

Jackson considered me. "Okay. I'll give you ten. But Merrick is forty points ahead of you, so you got some catching up to do. Oh, I know! You could start by looking at the man more than one time." His eyes got wide as he made his point. He gestured toward Atlas. I clenched my jaw, and he gestured again. I sighed in defeat.

When I turned to look at him this time, I pressed my lips together and sighed as I met his eyes. He seemed to be wrestling with something. He ran his hand through his hair in a frustrated type of gesture. I watched his movements with utter focus and curiosity. I felt my mouth relax as I let myself look at Atlas Merrick, the person, and not Atlas Merrick, the actor. That was the thing that had prompted me to write to him to begin with. I saw Atlas Merrick, the person, and though he was wonderful in his movies, he was profound as a person.

He settled himself into putting his arms on the table and leaning in a little. His focus remained on me, and I found myself curious to know why. Why come out here? Why search? Why seek to know? Why try to find?

He felt so familiar to me now. Like he was already a friend.

I quickly found that I no longer had a desire to look way. The more I saw him, the more I didn't care about whether or not I was seen by him. I turned my body in his direction so I could rest my elbow on the back of my seat and lean my head against my hand. There was something special about sharing a moment with another person that was simply about experiencing the other individual. And right now, in this moment, I found I appreciated him in a way I had not before that night in New York City.

A small smile blossomed on his face, and I found genuine joy that something had made him happy. His grief stayed with me long after that night. His smile reached into his eyes. He mouthed "hello," and I examined him further. I noted every detail. I watched the way he moved and the way his chest rose with his breath. He was careful but generous with the expressions on his face. His pale blue button-up denim shirt was unbuttoned at the collar, and the edges caught the breeze coming off the ocean. He had the sleeves rolled up almost to his elbows, and he was fidgeting with the spot he had rolled them up to.

My eyes returned to his, and I let him see my confusion. It wasn't just one thing I was confused by, it was many, and I think he could sense that by looking at me. I wanted to see inside of him. I wanted to understand the deeper complexities of who he was and the deeper aspects of what I already knew about him.

"Earth to Aria."

The sound of Jackson's voice made me jump. I dropped my hand from my lower lip and returned to face him. "Are you okay?" He was eyeing me with compassion and patience. All of his teasing was gone. I sniffled, not expecting to be having an emotional response. He handed me his napkin, and I wiped at the corners of my eyes. "What was that about?" His question wasn't invasive; it was patient.

I shook my head as I set the napkin down. "I... I don't know. I feel... I feel...."

"An unexpected connection?"

I laughed. "It doesn't make sense, right? I mean... it doesn't make sense." How could it make sense when Jackson didn't know some vital details of that unexpected connection?

Jackson leaned back in his seat. "How would I know how to make sense of all of this? How do any of us know? What I do know is you are a deep person. And from what I know about him, he is searching for those deep things about life. It seems like you two are like spirits. Like spirits are bound to find one another."

I grabbed the napkin and dabbed at my eyes again. "When did you get all wise on me?" I laughed through my tears. "This can't happen." I shook my head.

"Don't go destroying a beautiful thing before it's even taken flight," he cautioned me. He peaked at Atlas and his face lit with surprise. "Then again, you might not have a choice."

"What?"

His look of surprise had me looking back at Atlas, who was now walking our way.

I freaked.

"No. No Aria. Don't," he tried to stave off my panic, but it was too late. The adrenaline hit my system in a split second, and I was on my feet, already racing to leave. I very briefly caught the sight of Atlas breaking into a jog. "You're my ride!" Jackson's voice called after me.

"I'll text you where to meet me," I yelled back without looking.

the explanation

Jackson

"Oh man," Atlas muttered as he came to a full stop beside the chair she had been sitting in. He gripped the back edge of it.

"Have a seat," I said as I watched the disappointment on his face. He looked at me like that was the last thing in the world he wanted to do. He was frustrated, and I could tell if that man could chase her down, he would. "Just trust me. You're not going to catch up to her today."

He was hesitant but eventually took a seat in the chair she had occupied a short moment ago. "I wasn't expecting her to run. Not after she was so...."

"Direct with her gaze? Yeah. She has that effect on people," I commented.

He furrowed his eyebrows like he may be confused. "So, she does that a lot, then?"

I made a face at his question that I hoped conveyed he wasn't quite correct. "Well, she has a direct way of looking at people, yes, but from what I could tell, it was very different than her past experiences."

Atlas leaned on the table. "Why did she run then? You're friends with her, I'm guessing?"

I nodded. "Yup. Friends for... geez... a while. And she ran because you just being here freaked her out enough, but you trying to make contact with her in a more... meaningful way, let's say, that was like completely off the table."

Atlas laughed and nodded as he processed my words. "What's your name?"

"Jackson," I replied.

"Nice to meet you, Jackson. I'm afraid I may have just ruined everything I was planning to achieve just now."

"No. You didn't ruin it. You just have to give her time to adjust."

"How am I supposed to do that if she won't let me close to her?"

"Well, you can start by taking out your phone, so I can give you her number. I'll give you mine, too, in case you need insight into that complex mind of hers." Atlas raised his eyebrows and took out his phone, and I relayed the numbers to him. "Okay. Second thing. Next time you see her, don't give her so much space. She doesn't look like she can run fast, but when that adrenaline hits her system, she turns into the Road Runner in two seconds."

Atlas chuckled. "I can see that," he commented.

"And the third thing I will tell you, but I need you to answer a question for me first."

"Of course," he replied eagerly.

"Why are you here for her?"

He raised his eyebrows at my question and leaned back against the seat. "That's complicated."

I nodded. "If it helps simplify things, I know she sent you a letter, and I know the general concepts of the letter, and it doesn't surprise me that it would intrigue you," I supplied.

He nodded as his eyes widened a little bit. "It does help... a little."

"Okay. So, spill. I'm all ears," I said, cutting to the chase.

"Why am I here? Why am I here? How do I explain this?" He waited a moment, and then a look passed over his features like he finally had the answer he was looking for. "Have you ever connected with someone in a way that made you feel like you already knew them?" I chuckled as I looked down. "What's funny?"

I looked out at the ocean before looking back at him. "You sound like her."

His eyes brightened with interest. "Did she say that to you?"

"You'll have to find that out for yourself. So, third thing. You like the deeper aspects of life, yeah?"

"Absolutely," he replied.

"Lead with that stuff. It's the quickest way to get her not to react so abruptly. Say something that makes her stop and think, and you'll have a captive audience." My phone went off with a text notification. I picked it up. It was her. She had instructions on where to meet her. I shook my head and chuckled.

"It seems like you know her well," Atlas noted.

I looked back up at him. Was that a hint of something more that I detected? "We go back a way. I've seen her go through a lot."

"You weren't surprised she sent me the letter?"

I considered that for a moment. "No. Not really. She's not the kind of person that likes to live half a life, you know? She's more likely to take big risks. The risks that change life entirely. Now, the small stuff she will analyze until she completely tires herself out. Let me ask you a question. If there was one thing about the letter that you could say made you decide to try to find her, what would it be?"

His eyebrows lifted as he thought about my question. "One thing? There was so much. It's kind of difficult for me to narrow it down to one thing, at least in terms of the letter."

That was an odd statement, I thought to myself as Atlas leaned forward as he continued to think.

"I guess, if I had to pick one thing, it would be the way she views the power of love to completely change situations for the absolutely best outcome."

I smiled. "Yup. That's Aria."

Aria

I wasn't sure why I was back here.

It was a week after I had run out of here like the hounds of hell were chasing me down. Jackson had sent me a message a few hours ago asking what I was up to, and I told him I was coming back here. The beach next to the restaurant was beautiful, and there was something in me that just needed the peace that the ocean offered. He had asked me if everything was okay because he knew how I got in moments like this. I reassured him that I was, but everything inside of me was rattled.

As I walked down the beach and away from the outside patio of the restaurant, I looked up into the night sky. The stars were glittering back at me, and the moon beckoned me with her generous rays. I zipped up my dark blue hoodie and put my hands in the front pockets.

I stopped there and just listened to the waves dance along the shoreline. I closed my eyes and thought back to everything that had taken place a week ago. I was torn between feeling like I should not have run and feeling like I did the best thing in that moment. There was a part of me that wanted to know him. It was difficult to find someone so focused on the meaning of life in a world like this one. Everything was structured around doing and achieving and always pressing for more without thought or care to the heart of a person.

Seeing Atlas' take on the world and on what life is all about was like a healing balm to the soul after constantly being subjected to the things in life that seemed to lack compassion. It made the world feel so unwelcoming. It made it feel like the only way to survive it was to detach from it in as many ways as possible.

That was not a road I wanted to go back down.

He spoke to a deeper part of the human experience that I often thought about but rarely found others were thinking about. His words stayed with me long after his interviews were over. His intuitiveness was something I found myself completely amazed by. I needed to see someone like him. I needed that experience more than anyone would ever know. It made me feel hopeful when the world was currently offering up so little hope.

I sat on the sandy shore and pulled my hoodie up. I closed my eyes and took in the beautiful simplicity of the moment. I needed this. I needed to feel somehow connected to this world despite the fact that I felt such a lack of connection to so much of the world.

Maybe it wasn't fair of me, but writing to him had been something I had to do. I couldn't stop myself from doing it. The words had bled out of me and onto paper. Everything I wanted to say, everything I needed to say, the connection I had to make; all of it was beyond my ability to contain. I was really good at self-control. Probably much better than most people realize. But not in this. This had been beyond my ability to control. After holding it all in for so long, I found myself asking the question, did I really want to hold it all in?

Everything about the situation with Atlas felt like the perfect way to express what I needed to express. It felt safe to do so. I could pour out my heart and pray that he received it with a measure of understanding and that he could take things away from it that he would find edifying, and I wouldn't have to worry about anything after that. The pressure would leave me, and I would continue on as I always had, walking through life half-alive.

It was not the way life should be lived, but it was the way I had to live it.

A movement to my right caught my attention as someone in long, light tan shorts and a dark blue hoodie sat down on the sand not more than ten feet away from me. I couldn't make out much of the person as their hood was pulled up and covering their features. I could tell from his form, in general, that he was a man. He put his arms over his knees. "Do you come out here often?" His voice. I would always know it.

"Uh… not as much as I'd like to, I suppose," I replied. There was no use running.

"Too many demands on your time?"

That was an interesting way to put it. "Something like that. But don't we all have demands on our time? I should make the time. That and… turn off my phone."

"Phones do seem to be both a blessing and a curse," he supplied.

"That they do. It feels good to detach from all the noise and all of the demands," I sighed as I looked up at the moon. "I miss the simplicity of life." Out of the corner of my eye, I saw Atlas turn toward me, and I tried to turn and catch a glimpse of his face, but he moved too quickly for me to see it. "It feels like people found a way to occupy every single second of their time, and I find it has left me feeling exhausted. Where's the room to explore all the things in life that hold the greatest meaning?"

I sighed.

"I'm sorry. I didn't mean to get all personal," I said as I looked back to the moon and the stars.

"Don't apologize. I couldn't agree with you more. After New York City, I don't think you should worry about getting personal," he commented. He followed up with a question. "May I ask you a question?"

I let my eyes stay on him for a moment before I finally turned my attention back to the night sky. "Yes."

"What, in life, do you believe holds the greatest meaning?"

I didn't even have to think about what my answer was. I already knew what it was. I had thought about it over and over.

"In a word… love. It never ceases to amaze me how one word can have so much meaning."

"Or how often people don't utilize its effectiveness."

I turned to look at him again, but he was still in that same position facing forward. "It seems like the world is starved for it, don't you think?" He picked up something next to him and threw it in the water. "Do you ever wonder, if all of humanity came to a stop for a full day, how many people would weep from carrying pressure they never gave themselves proper time to release?"

Just like that, I was thrown back five weeks, and I was back in that apartment as I remembered how much his grief had overtaken him.

"I never had the opportunity to get your name that night," he said as he let me hear the saturation of sadness in his voice.

"You must know it now," I finally said.

"I do. Aria. I like that name."

"Can we just go back to the way it was before? Where you don't know my name and I'm not distracted by yours?"

"After what happened in New York City, why would you be distracted by my name?"

He turned his head toward me and pushed the hood of his hoodie back.

I stared at Atlas at a complete loss as to what I should do. Part of me was desperate to run, but he was directly in my exit path. I looked away from him as a tear slid effortlessly from my eye to get lost in the fabric of my hoodie. I looked back at the night sky and sighed as I replayed our current conversation in my head.

Then I got to remembering the letter. My heart started to race.

"You seem calmer," he noted.

I laughed. "Appearances can be deceiving," I responded as I pulled the sleeves of my hoodie over my hands.

"You don't want to be seen, but you crave genuine connection," he observed. His observation nearly knocked the breath right out of my lungs.

"I don't want to be seen because it seems like the human race has forgotten how delicate the spirit is. And... I'm not the only one who craves connection."

"True, but I'm not sure I know many people that crave the kind of connection you do," he observed.

Goosebumps erupted all over my skin as I tried to process and get used to the unfamiliar sensation of being truly seen and understood by another person. I tried to be nonchalant. I turned to look at him. I had a moment of all of this feeling so surreal. "You mean the kind of connection that life should be about?"

"It's more than that," he answered.

"I don't know if I want to talk about this," I quickly responded.

"I'm actually surprised you haven't tried to run yet," he said.

I looked pointedly over his shoulder. "Kind of blocking my exit there, Atlas." I winced as I said his name. "Oh gosh. I never asked you if you are okay with me calling you by your first name."

He tilted his head like he was trying to open himself up to me more. "Yes, you absolutely can call me by my first name."

I rubbed at a spot on my forehead like I could rub away this whole situation somehow. "It seems so informal."

"Between your letter and New York, I think we probably settled the issue of formalities," he replied with a light chuckle.

I groaned because I really didn't want to be in this situation. I really didn't want to talk about all of this. I wanted to go back to being unseen. Well, part of me did. There was another part of me that was afraid of the feeling that was stirring in me. It was that feeling of relief. Relief that there was someone out there who saw things in a similar way as I did.

"May I... may I come closer?"

He was so considerate that I found it really difficult to say no to him. I didn't want him far away, but I worried about the effect he would have on me with him being closer. I knew myself well enough to know that I would seek that connection we found in New York. I would want to stay inside that space for as long as I possibly could. And I knew him enough to know that he would take no issue staying in that space with me.

But I wasn't the same person I had been those many weeks ago. I didn't have the same courage. I didn't feel the same bravery. I was bogged down by the weight of the world again. And his world was so different than mine.

"I really don't know," I said honestly.

I looked into his brown eyes, hoping he could see how sorry I was about that answer. He raised his eyebrows like he had an idea, and everything about his expression very much indicated that the ball was in my court, and he did not want to come off as threatening in any way. "How about... just a little closer. I'd like to see your face better if I could."

"If you're going to gauge my reactions, I must warn you; I can't make promises. Sometimes, I'm as much of a blank slate on the outside as what I feel on the inside," I warned.

"You can be whatever you need to be. I just want to be closer so I can see it more clearly." His voice was so soft and so non-threatening. How was I supposed to say no?

I couldn't say no.

"Okay," I relented in a soft whisper.

The moment he stood to his feet, it felt like my foundation went out from underneath me. I felt the panic rising as the adrenaline laced my blood within a split second. I dug my hands into the sand, and I wasn't sure if I was doing that to keep myself there or to prepare to push myself to my feet and get the heck out of there.

He took one step and stopped. He raised his hands and waited for me to look at him. "How's this?" He asked with a smirk.

The tension in my shoulders evaporated, and I laughed. He was teasing me. "Gee, I don't know, Mr. Merrick... you're really pressing your luck."

He chuckled and waited a moment, clearly letting me be the one to decide what would happen next.

I met his friendly brown eyes. "Just come as close as you want," I relented. "Just don't judge me if I get antsy."

He didn't wait for me to second-guess myself. He immediately moved closer until a foot separated us. I felt myself go ridged as he sat down next to me. "For the record," he started as he settled himself beside me. "You may have moments where you feel like a blank slate, but I can say with confidence that is not at all what you are."

I felt the warmth coming from him, from his body, from his soul, from his spirit. And all of it was so welcoming I found myself fighting its gravitational pull on me. I closed my eyes and tried to focus on control.

Control.

Control.

Control.

"Please, say something to distract me because it sort of feels like a supernova is about to happen in me," I said, like I was hopped up on way too much caffeine. Thank you, adrenaline.

Not.

"I enjoyed the process of trying to find you," he said gently.

The storm settled, and I turned to meet his eyes. I expected to be completely thrown off by his proximity, but I found his nearness had the opposite effect. I settled down, and my spirit eased as I looked at him. "Can I ask you a question?" He nodded as he assessed my face. "This might sound... unusual, but may I just assess you for a moment?"

His eyes were moving rapidly over my face as I spoke, but I saw his surprise and curiosity as his eyes finally came back to mine. He nodded again. "Like you did last week?"

I shook my head as I started to absorb the details of his features. "No," I whispered. "More." He nodded again, and we both let silence wrap around us. It wasn't just about me assessing him. He was assessing me and processing my reactions to him at the same time. Everything about him was familiar; the dark brown stylish hair, the trimmed beard, the slight edge to his jaw. But that wasn't what made it feel like I knew him.

I met his eyes, and the experience changed. There was this look he had in his eyes that reflected knowledge, understanding, humbleness, and compassion. It was a look that assured you that you were seen by him and not overlooked. I'm sure there was a look of pure wonder that I wore because that was exactly how I felt right now.

There were so many people I interacted with on a daily basis. There was so much need that I met for others. There were so many people I offered my comfort to without ever receiving comfort in return. I often acted like a well for thirsty people, but my well was running dry. I had nothing left to give.

I felt a tear escape. His eyes caught the event but quickly returned to my eyes. "May I... this might sound odd, but may I touch your face for a moment?"

His eyes quickly roamed my face to absorb my expression. "Yes," he answered quickly.

I reached up and took comfort in knowing that my hand was pretty steady. I gently touched his temple and his cheek under his eye. The look in his eyes changed. He was very curious. He was open and accepting.

"Such wisdom," I whispered. I couldn't keep my surprise from mixing with my wonder. I stayed like that for a moment and watched as his eyes began to water. I finally moved my hand away and gave him a warm smile. My soul felt like it had gained a measure of peace. "Thank you," I said softly.

"You're so different," he said as he tried to maintain eye contact with me as I was in the process of looking down.

"Is that why you're here, Atlas?" I looked up and into the vast expanse of the ocean. I could see no end to it being as dark as it now was.

"I'm here because I didn't even know someone like you existed and when I read your letter, it spoke to so many things inside of me, and I just couldn't let you go after what happened in New York. I knew I had to talk to you. And I knew that I just wanted to listen to you. I knew that I… I wanted to comfort you. You gave me more than you could possibly know that night in New York," he finished.

I closed my eyes against the light of the full moon.

"Why did you leave, Aria?"

"It was the direction I was given by the Lord." I looked back into his eyes. I had missed those eyes these past weeks. "Only God can heal the kind of pain you endured when your mother passed," I said sympathetically.

"I understand that, and I agree with you, but having you there when I woke up would have helped me too."

I shook my head and grabbed at the sand. "It's easy for me to follow the will of the Lord when it is so directly given to me, but it's not easy to remain in a situation without Him. What would I have said? What would I have done?" I shook my head. "I won't disobey Him, Atlas. I did that once, and I grieved over that decision for months."

"I wouldn't ask that of you. I wasn't ready to say good-bye. I didn't get to say good-bye," he said.

Silence fell between us, and the weight of everything that had happened to get us both to this point weighed heavily upon me in this moment. I prayed the Lord would help guide me in this discussion, but I knew there was yet more to be revealed in this. I waited until I couldn't wait any longer.

"Did you find healing, Atlas?"

When his answer did not come, I looked back to meet his dark eyes. Even in the moonlight, I could see how rich the brown of his eyes was. He shook his head to indicate no to my question. "I'm trying. I'm trying to lean into God again, but I feel like I am in a lifeboat in the middle of an ocean with no land in sight," he said.

I watched him run his hand through the dark strands of his hair, displaying his frustration. "Please," he whispered after a moment. His tears were illuminated by the light of the moon. His lip quivered as he let me see his soul in his eyes. "Please, let me have this." He gestured between us.

"Atlas, I live in a very different world than you do. If I'm not built for a world falling into darkness, what makes you think I can withstand the kind of world you inhabit? I want to be your friend. Believe me," I pleaded with him as I fought against my warring emotions. "I want to help you. After the darkness you drew me out of, you have no idea how much I want to help you, but I don't know if I can handle it."

"I can protect you," he said.

"What is it you envision exactly, Atlas? Did you not see the pictures on the internet from that night? I was quite fortunate that whoever got the pictures was not able to get a picture of my face, or my life would be turned upside down right now."

Somehow, someone had gotten a picture of me cradled in the arms of Chase after my assault. People who ran in those circles knew Chase worked as a regular on Atlas' security detail, so they immediately made the connection between Atlas and me. Boy, had the rumors flown around like crazy. They were still whispering about it, but there was so much stuff going on in the world that the story had finally started to dissipate.

"I saw the pictures. I heard the rumors. I've learned how to handle it, but I can understand how upsetting it must be for you. I can still protect you, though," he said as his eyes continued to search mine. "You asked me what I envision. You not running away from me would be an ideal start," he answered me.

I winced as I attempted to turn my body toward him. He saw my expression change to one reflecting pain. Concern lit his eyes. He waited for me to tell him what had caused me pain, but I hesitated. "Tell me," he finally whispered after he couldn't tolerate the silence any longer. I pressed my lips together as I hesitated. "Please," he whispered.

"I went to the hospital when I returned from New York. The pain was really bad. They did x-rays and found two cracked ribs and a broken rib," I finished with a sigh.

He shook his head back and forth like doing so could make the truth somehow go away. "I'm so sorry. I should have made you go to the hospital that night. Please forgive me for my thoughtlessness."

I smiled at him. "Don't apologize, Atlas. It was my choice. I chose not to spend my time waiting in a hospital for God only knows how long. I knew the right choice. The right choice was to be there for you. I couldn't stand to constantly see that pain reflected in your eyes and not be able to do anything to try to help you."

"I'm still in pain; you're still in pain. So, close your eyes and tell me what you think God would have you do in this moment?" he said with exasperation.

I knew he was upset by many things. Part of me knew when I had seen him at that restaurant that it would come to this. The clash was inevitable. The war of wills was a fate that was sealed the moment I sat in that movie theater in November and watched him in that movie.

Even though I knew he was goading me, I did as he instructed. I waited for a moment to clear my mind. I let my senses numb as I focused on connecting to the Lord. *What would You have me do?*

It took several minutes of meditation with the Lord before I finally saw the answer flash before my eyes. That was the first time He had ever given me a vision. I hadn't expected it, but because of how much He spoke to me with dreams and in all of the research I had done, I knew that is precisely what had just happened.

I gasped as I finally opened my eyes and looked at the grief on Atlas' face. The grief melted as a look of recognition crossed over his features. "What did you see," he gently inquired.

"You're in so much pain," I whispered as I felt my face melt with compassion. I reached out to him, and he found my embrace much as he had that night in New York. I held him as he wept.

"Please," he whispered into the base of my neck. "I can't do this on my own."

I felt a shift in my spirit, and I knew what the Lord would want me to do. I couldn't leave Atlas to suffer his despair in silence. The Lord had sent me into Atlas' world to help him. I took a moment to remember how much God had used Atlas to pull me out of my wilderness. I had told Atlas the watered-down version of that season, but when I closed my eyes, I could still feel the loneliness and the darkness I had felt in those many months. I trembled at the memory.

"Are you cold?" he whispered as he tried to reign in his emotions. He wouldn't break his hold on me, though.

I shook my head. "No. No, I am not cold. And you will never have to do this on your own," I promised him as I held him. "I have no idea what happens next, Atlas, but I do know that you do not have to do this on your own."

the transparent

I was waiting for word from Atlas. He was supposed to meet me this evening, but his promise of 5 p.m. had come and gone some time ago. I checked my phone to see if I had any missed calls or text messages from him. There was nothing.

I already had significant reservations about Atlas meeting me at my apartment. With his notoriety came attention, and attention was not what I wanted. I considered it too risky. He was very well known, and I craved the comfort of smaller circles. Before we parted last night, he had promised me that he could keep his presence here under wraps.

I was grateful for his thoughtfulness and appreciated his sincerity, but I wondered how he would be able to keep such a promise. There were times in life when, despite our best efforts or noble intentions, some things just had a way of happening whether we wanted them to or not. I had relented, though. My compassion for his plight far outweighed my own self-interest.

I thought back to what the Lord had shown me. Atlas had asked me what I had seen, but I couldn't tell him. What I had come to learn was that there were many times in life when the Lord would move, but the time for the revealing of God's greater purpose needed space to fully manifest.

If I closed my eyes, I could still see what the Lord had shown me. I could still see Atlas starring into that mirror in his bathroom at his apartment in New York City. I could still see how hard he had gripped the edge of the dark granite countertop of his sink. I could see the quiver of his bottom lip as he tried to pull back on his emotions. I could see the tears swimming in his eyes.

It had been just a brief snapshot, but it had been accompanied by a wealth of knowledge from the Lord. It wasn't just about the physical manifestation of his pain that I could so clearly see. It was also the understanding that it was not just his mother's passing that he carried as a burden. His shoulders slumped with the weight of a new burden. It was a burden I had put on him.

I sighed.

That had not been my intention. I sought obedience to the Lord. I had not meant to add any further stress on a plate that was already full.

I had sought the Lord regarding this new information He had shown me. I had poured out my heart with tears that reflected the new element of pain that had been added to this whole situation because of my actions. It took some time for the Holy Spirit to settle me, but when I was finally settled, the Lord revealed a greater truth to me. It was something I needed to understand better before moving forward.

There were times in life when the Lord would use us to achieve a greater outcome. In those times of transition, there often was a greater shuffling that took place. The deeper truth was that sometimes the shaking itself looked bad on the surface, but God deconstructs the walls we build around ourselves to achieve greater works.

Was there ever a deconstruction process that looked pretty?

Every part of a process of deconstruction was riddled with imperfections along the way. It wasn't designed to be pretty. It was designed to take down the things that stood in the way of a person and God. Why did God do this? It had been my experience that at least one reason behind it was to root out the unrighteous things that created chasms between a person and God.

The burden that had been created when I left New York was meant to be there. It had been designed to do two things; help Atlas acknowledge his pain and help Atlas seek after the solution found only in the Lord. Every step in that process mattered. Every action taken held the promise of fruitful outcomes if we could look with clear eyes and an open heart at what good could come from it all.

My phone went off in my purse. I looked at the screen on my phone. There was a message from him waiting for me.

ATLAS: *Running late. Sorry. I'll be there shortly.*

Shortly turned into an hour later.

I opened my apartment door to find Atlas on the phone. Behind him stood two members of his security team. I met Chase's eyes as Atlas turned to face me. He held up one finger to me to indicate he would be done in a moment. I nodded and moved out of the way so he could make his way in.

I watched Atlas pace my kitchen while his security team came in. Atlas' dark blue shirt stood out in sharp contrast to the white cabinets of my kitchen. He put his free hand in the pocket of his light denim jeans and shrugged a shoulder at me, and mouthed, "I'm sorry." A smile was my response.

I offered Chase and the other man some drinks and set out some snacks on the coffee table in the living room. I opened the balcony doors to let in the breeze coming in from the ocean. I then went to sit down across from Chase.

The look in his eyes seemed so similar to the one he had when he left Atlas' apartment that night five weeks ago. I couldn't make out the complexity of his inner turmoil, but I could clearly see his struggle with that turmoil.

"You seem different," he started.

I shrugged my shoulders in a dismissive way. I very rarely lent too much power to the turmoil these days. It was too heavy of a burden for me to bear. I took time to process it, but I was careful never to let it gain too much momentum. I found that if that turmoil gained too much momentum, it could quickly turn into a root of pain that would only do more damage later. God wants us healed from pain, not carrying the weight of it.

"You seem... sadder," I commented.

Chase looked away from me. The way he held his eyes spoke to the manifestation of his memories. "Well, justice has its consequences," he sighed.

I felt a strange stirring in my spirit. It didn't feel good. *Justice has consequences?* I remembered how shaken up Chase had been after he had stopped my attackers those many weeks ago. I remembered our conversation in the vehicle as we'd made our way to Atlas' apartment. I could still see the frustration in his blue eyes.

"Chase," I spoke his name just above a whisper. When his eyes finally met mine, they were red with unshed tears. I always found tears a beautiful thing. They had a way of highlighting the color of a person's eyes and always spoke to great strength in the vulnerability it takes for those tears to come forward and fall.

"What did you do?" I asked. He didn't even blink at my question, but I could see the weight of that unspoken thing reflecting in his eyes. I noted how stiff his posture was and the tension that was in his jaw as he pressed his lips together.

"I'm so sorry," Atlas addressed me as he came over and ended his phone call. I met his eyes, though the weight of the burden Chase was clearly carrying was the dominant thing in my mind at the moment. Atlas took a seat next to me. "Someone caught wind that I was here in town, so I was working with my public relations team to try to fix it. I didn't want to leave until I thought it would be safe to do so without risking someone following us," he finished.

The image the Lord had shown me last night while Atlas and I had sat on the beach came to the forefront of my mind. I gave him a warm smile as I remembered how much pain there was in his eyes in the vision I had seen. "I would like to continue our conversation from last night," he said. His eyes met mine as he waited for me to agree.

I was grateful for the opportunity, but after seeing the look in Chase's eyes, I knew he needed to unburden himself. If that burden wasn't so dominant in him, then he wouldn't have been on the verge of breaking down just a moment ago.

Chase got up abruptly, muttered something about checking outside, and disappeared out onto the balcony.

I met Atlas' brown eyes. "I think I need to talk with Chase for just a moment. Is that okay?"

Atlas drew his eyebrows together. "Of course. Is everything okay?" He looked to where Chase had just made his exit and then back to me.

"I'm not quite sure," I replied. I got up and went out onto the balcony.

Chase had been leaning against the rail with his forearms but quickly stood to his full height upon seeing me.

I assessed him.

"Don't look at me like that," he said as he looked toward the open expanse of the ocean.

Though his tone was defensive, I took no personal offense to it. "Whatever happened... you don't have to carry the weight of it alone," I said.

He shook his head at me. "All I did was administer a little justice. Eye for an eye, right?" When he finally looked back at me, his eyes were like stone.

I didn't respond right away, and instead, I reflected on how much pain perpetrates more pain. In both un-suspecting ways and in ways that are entirely predictable, pain perpetrates more pain. The night I was attacked, this was essentially what I had been trying to warn Chase away from by highlighting the importance of forgive-ness. Hurt people have a tendency to hurt other people. Pain, left unresolved, would find ways to the surface and impact other people. I hadn't spent enough time helping Chase with his pain.

"Whatever you have done... don't let it bury you. It can stop here. It can end now. It can be different going forward. If you want it to be that way," I said. I waited patiently as he thought about what I had said.

"I thought if I could right a wrong, that it would make me feel better. Like I could somehow fix the injustice by taking action against it," he finally said.

"What happened, Chase?"

He shrugged his shoulders. "I tracked them down, at least the ones whose faces I could remember, let them toss me up a bit to give me an excuse to toss them up a bit. I called the police ahead of time so by the time they got there, they would find the guys who hurt you tossing me up."

I took a deep breath and held it as I thought about what he had just shared with me. What would the Lord have me say in this moment? I didn't want Chase to feel condemned because that's not what the Lord would want him to feel. The Lord would want him to be free from the prison that pain puts people in.

"Do you know about Jesus from the Bible?"

Chase shook his head "no" at me and went to lean his forearms against the rail of the balcony again. I wasn't sure how much of this he would entertain, but I was hopeful that maybe something about this would help him. I mimicked Chase's posture as I began to speak to him.

"Jesus was born in a time of great darkness. He's part of the divine trinity of God; God the Father, God the Son, and God the Holy Spirit. God the Son is Jesus Christ. From the beginning, Jesus was to be the atoning sacrifice for the sin of mankind. He was born of the virgin Mary. At the appointed time, He began to minister to the lost that He was the way to the Father. He performed great and numerous miracles before He went to the cross. He was crucified. He took on the burden of sin, and we now have the precious gift of grace and a way to connect back to the Father. It took a long time for me to be able to understand a fraction of the love it took for Christ to suffer the way He did and yet still choose the cross so we could have a way back to the Father."

Chase looked at me then and gave me a small smile. "Is that what I see in you, then? Reflections of Jesus?"

I lowered my head. "The walk of a Christian is not easy. It is challenging. If we are fortunate enough to grab hold of the promises of God, then our lives can and should reflect the nature of Christ. Even though it is challenging, it is the greatest journey in life. It has the potential to bring forward so many blessings and establish a joy inside that nothing else in life can replicate. If you see an element of Jesus in me, then please know that I find that a humbling thing."

"Why do you tell me all of this?"

"The burdens of life are too numerous for us to handle alone. People need one another. These days are not for the faint of heart, and there are many opportunities to change things for the better. There are many opportunities for us to grab a hold of those promises God has given us and to encourage one another in the love He demonstrates to us in so many ways. We have unique opportunities to uplift one another, to encourage one another, and to demonstrate love and compassion to one another. All we have to do is choose that. It is a choice that is constantly ours to make. It is filled with promises that are constantly set out on the table for us to take," I said with a smile. I hoped he could see the compassion I had for him.

"I understand your points, but it's not making it easier for me to make peace with what happened," he said as he wiped tears from his eyes.

"Only Jesus can do that. He is the only One who has the authority to bridge the gap between God and us so we can find true forgiveness. He suffered the penalty of sin when He went to the cross. He made the offer of salvation for anyone who chooses Him. It's an offer only He can give and a decision that only you can make," I finished softly.

While silence took over, Chase's tears came harder. "I don't want to live with this guilt," his words forced themselves from him as he broke down.

I went over to him and put my hand on his shoulder. "You don't have to, Chase. If you choose to give your life to Jesus, then you can be free. You can have eternity with the Creator of everything who sacrificed Himself and died for you. The One who took your sin and paid the price for it on the cross. You can have true freedom, Chase."

He turned to me and wrapped me in a hug as his body was wracked with the tremors of the guilt he was living with. I wished I had stopped to consider the consequences of that night more thoroughly. But even in the bad parts of that night, here God was moving in the aftermath to bring about something beautiful. I hoped that Chase chose that precious gift that only God could give him through Jesus Christ.

Chase held on to me like I was a lifeline. I let him. If an anchor was what he needed, then I would be happy to be that for him until he could find the true anchor we all needed.

It took some time for Chase to settle down. It was only when Atlas came out to check on us that Chase abruptly released me, stepped away, and righted himself. He turned away so Atlas couldn't see his face. I smiled at Atlas and told him I would be right in.

Chase looked back at me after Atlas went back inside. "Can I think about what you said?"

I nodded immediately at his question. "Of course. In the meantime, come inside and know that my home is yours. Let it be your sanctuary. Your place to find a measure of peace," I said as I smiled.

"I don't deserve your kindness," he replied.

"It's not about what we deserve. It's about holding onto a love that is far greater than any of us can fully comprehend on this side of heaven. It's about letting that love impact every part of our lives. And knowing that when we make that decision to surrender our lives to Jesus and ask Him to be the Lord of our lives that we get to live a life of redemption every day."

He came up to me and hugged me again. "Please, don't go anywhere this time," he whispered in my ear.

I nodded against as best as I could. "I'm here for you," I responded.

He released his hold on me, and we both went back inside.

Atlas stood up as soon as we entered.

I smiled at him and wondered if I would ever get used to seeing him dressed more casual than formal. His jeans and dark blue shirt were such a difference from the dress suits he wore to events in Hollywood.

Atlas motioned to the other person on his team who was sitting on the couch. Without a word, the person stood up, and he and Chase went to the kitchen to sit at the island. I took an empty spot on the couch so I could be directly across from Atlas.

"I have questions," he stated.

"I hope to provide you with answers," I replied.

He rolled up the sleeves of his shirt and leaned forward with his elbows on his knees. I remembered the dichotomy of Atlas' gaze that night five weeks ago. He'd been both direct and indirect. Now, he seemed to be interested in simply being direct.

"That depiction of Jesus in the Garden that you wrote in your letter," he stated simply and let his sentence go unfinished. He waited patiently for me to take hold of the reigns he had just handed to me.

"The only thing that was powerful enough to take the pain away," I stated simply.

"What happened?"

"The details, in the grand scheme of the event itself, are not as impactful as what happened in the aftermath. It's simple looking back on it, but it was a fight to get through each day of it at the time. It's in those moments of our greatest struggle that we can connect to Jesus in ways we could never dream of, and in ways we wouldn't be able to without the event itself," I finished. "If we let ourselves, that is," I said as an afterthought.

Atlas' eyes remained on mine like he was trying to find out more details just by looking at me. "You didn't resent what happened because of the pain it caused you?" I immediately saw the deeper truth he was searching for inside his question.

"Resent? No. First and foremost, the pain from the injury was far too dominant for me to be focused at all on resentment. More important than that, though, is that I knew resentment would be a waste of precious energy, and it was energy I didn't have to spend on that. Everything in my life was upended in one second. When simple movements are no longer attainable, everything becomes centered around figuring out how to function. You relearn your physical parameters because they are suddenly entirely different."

Atlas drew his eyebrows together like he was searching for understanding but had trouble finding it. I watched his reactions closely. I measured my next words before continuing.

"The day I wrote that depiction of Jesus in the Garden, I was fighting against a significant amount of physical pain. Nothing I did was able to keep the pain at bay, so I closed my eyes, and I visualized myself with Jesus in the moments of His greatest struggle. I wasn't afraid of the knowledge of His struggle. Sometimes, the truth of what Jesus endured can be overwhelming, and I have encountered moments in my life where it was overwhelming for me to attempt to understand. Once I started learning about His love, then, my perception of His sacrifice started to change. I wasn't so focused on His pain as I was on how much love He had to do what He did for us. I knew I didn't know nearly enough about the power that was behind His sacrifice, so I dedicated myself to learning."

"Is the mark on your neck from the event that caused you so much pain?"

I looked back at Atlas, unable to keep my shock contained. No one had ever seen the mark on my neck without me directly pointing it out to them. It was an internal injury that could only be felt or seen if I moved in a specific direction. He was the only one who had observed me enough to see it on his own.

"What is it? Why are you looking at me like that?"

"Yes, the mark on my neck is from that event," I answered his original question. "I'm just a little surprised at how intuitive you are, but I shouldn't be surprised. The way you observe the world and the people around you were the first things that caught my attention about you."

He broke eye contact with me to look down at the coffee table that separated us from one another. "And the scars on your shoulder... are those from the event?" I watched his movements closely. There was often much that could be learned in taking time to observe a person, and sometimes, it ended up being more informative than the communication found in the exchanging of words.

"Yes. Surgical scars," I elaborated further for him.

He must have noticed them the night we met.

His eyes met mine on the wings of another question. "And placing yourself with Jesus in His suffering was the only thing that helped you manage the pain?"

"Jesus said His yoke was easy, and His burden was light. I put myself in what I thought was His most vulnerable moment because I was in my most vulnerable moment. I knew no one would be able to understand what I was going through because there is no way for us to truly and fully understand another person's pain because we don't have full access to the heart of another person. The only One that does is Christ. I knew that no one would be able to understand better than Him."

I watched tears form in Atlas' eyes, and I knew he was gaining something in this moment. My hope was that it was something that could help heal some of the damage his heart had sustained with the loss of his mother.

"And it worked?"

I leaned forward so Atlas could gauge my reactions and my words with more precision. "You are in the Garden with Jesus." I began.

A tear slipped over the rim of his eye as awareness of what I was doing dawned on the features of his face. He covered his mouth with his hand as a quiver began in his lips. I watched him as his breathing became uneven. Despite his inner turmoil, he waited patiently for me to continue.

"You watch as Jesus sweats blood because His body is bearing the weight of your sin. You are in the Garden with Jesus. Looking into His eyes, you feel the enormity of His love for you. You take each step with Him as He makes His way to the cross. You are on His mind as He is nailed to that unspeakably beautiful cross. You are on His mind as He pays the price that no one else can pay for you. He is willing to pay this price for you because He loves you so much."

Atlas' bravery was beautiful. He didn't look away from me despite the tears that spilled from his eyes. He wasn't distracted by his own vulnerabilities.

"Jesus is with you in the loss of your mother. Jesus is with you in your despair. Jesus is with you in your frustrations and the grief of your heart," I said softly.

Atlas abruptly stood up and approached me. "Please, stand," he said as he stood still before me. I looked up at him, trying to understand what I was witnessing. "Please stand, Aria," he repeated.

I stood up and was better able to assess his internal struggle in a way I had not been able to before.

"I need you to promise me something," Atlas said as he searched my eyes to measure my reaction. Normally, I did not make promises without understanding what I would be promising, but I had such a strong stirring in my spirit to agree. I nodded in response to him.

"Promise me you won't disappear on me again. Please," he finished. I hesitated, but it was not because I wasn't willing to make that promise to him. I hesitated because there was so much going on in him that I was trying to fully observe, and it was distracting me from answering him.

"Please. You would agree that Christians need one another, right? Especially with everything going on in the world right now?" I nodded to him. "Then, please, promise me because I am not too proud to say that I need you. I don't know how else to say it other than to say that you are like a kindred spirit to me."

I smiled at his sincerity, and I understood that need to find like-minded people and how important that was in this world that was growing darker. "I promise," I whispered. Atlas immediately wrapped me in a hug.

Even if Atlas and I were separated in this life due to the unpredictability of this world, we would be reunited the moment it was finally time for Jesus to intervene in the affairs of mankind, as He promised us repeatedly in the Scriptures that He would do one day.

That was a day Christians everywhere were looking forward to with great expectancy in our hearts.

the pressure

A tlas was gone.
Chase was gone.

I was alone once more.

I felt their loss, like I had temporarily lost a part of myself. There was more work to be done. There was more healing that needed to take place. I thought back to Chase specifically as I knew he was contending with what he had done in a way that he had not been able to fully reconcile yet. He hadn't accepted Jesus yet. With the world growing more unstable and more unpredictable, I carried the burden to further witness Christ to Chase, and it was a burden for the lost to be saved that grew stronger with each passing day.

Atlas had needed to go back to Los Angeles for some reshoots of his latest work. He promised to stay in touch with me and that he would return as soon as he could. Chase had given me a somber smile and a hug that didn't seem to really connect the way a hug was designed to connect.

My heart grieved for him.

It was already challenging enough to have so much unfinished work. It became much more challenging when I went on the internet and saw my face on way too many websites. I stared at the picture of me and Atlas that had clearly been taken on the day he left. This time, the connection between Atlas and me was undeniable, as the picture clearly displayed our departing hug.

It was easy to make out the details of my face.

There was a part of me that hoped that it would just be a fleeting story that not many people would be interested in. There was another part of me that found it highly unlikely that there would not be any after-effects of that picture being across the internet. It remained to be seen if there would be after-effects and, if there were, what they would look like.

The first time I noticed that something was not right was while returning home from work one night. At first, I dismissed the idea that the black SUV behind me was following me. I thought it was merely notable that it seemed to be staying close to me while I drove on the highway. But, every time I switched lanes, the driver of that SUV would switch lanes.

I couldn't see into the windows, even with the setting sun shining upon the SUV. I couldn't even see the driver. I pulled off the highway at my normal exit, and the SUV did the same.

That's when I had a check in my spirit that something was not right. I prayed and hoped that the release of adrenaline from my body would not overpower my need to connect to the Holy Spirit. I'd been in situations before where adrenaline and the fear response clouded my ability to tie into the guidance of the Holy Spirit. It took discipline to counter the response of the flesh so I could more clearly feel God's guidance.

The SUV turned in the same direction I turned.

I could feel the fight or flight response kicking in, but I immediately countered it by voicing my prayer to the Lord. There was such power in using your voice in prayer. It helped to focus the mind on a task. It helped eliminate the power of distractions.

The Book of Genesis tells of how God spoke creation into existence. If we are made in His likeness and image, just as the Bible says we are, then that means we, too, have power in what we speak. The Bible tells us the power of life and death is in the tongue. Then, it goes on to tell us to choose life.

That means that what we speak matters. How often do we treat that truth with the seriousness that it deserves? How often do we speak words of life over someone who is in need of edification? How often do we give the measure of love that is in our hearts to others who are in despair? Do we recognize their longing? Do we recognize the desperation of their need? How often are people unable to put words to what it is they long for?

I often thought to myself that there is a hole inside each one of us, a precious and sacred space that only God Himself can fill. Only one name can be written there. Only one can claim that spot.

Jesus Christ.

Pondering these things helped to ease some of the adrenaline response from my body as I continued on my path to my apartment. I let my voice carry throughout the confines of my car as the SUV continued to follow me.

I didn't pull into the parking lot of my apartment complex. I continued to drive and decided to pass by the apartments and go to a local diner to see what would happen. A public place would be the best kind of surrounding to determine the intent of the driver of the SUV.

I arrived at the diner a short time later. The SUV pulled into the same parking lot as I did. As soon as I got out of my car, all of the doors of the SUV opened, and a whirlwind of activity rushed at me. Out rushed people with cameras of various sizes. They approached me so quickly I had trouble catching up with what was happening.

I lifted my hands over my face as flashes from cameras made my eyes sensitive.

"Aria, when did you and Atlas start seeing each other?"

"Aria, are you and Atlas together?"

"How did you and Atlas meet?"

"Aria, do you miss Atlas? Are you going to go see him? When is he back coming to see you?"

As the questions swarmed at me, I felt my heartbeat quicken and was immediately grateful that I had driven past my apartment to a public place instead. The last thing I wanted was for the paparazzi to discover where I lived. Though I highly doubted I would be able to keep my address private for long now that Atlas and I were connected in the eyes of the public.

I lowered my hands from my face as the lights from their cameras continued to flash in my eyes.

"Please respect my privacy," I stated softly as they continued to take pictures of me. I realized quickly that my request was not going to be honored. I looked at one of the lenses that I gathered was likely recording me. "Atlas," I whispered as I looked directly into the lens.

I broke through the group of people and ran down the street. I passed several businesses and ran down some alleys until I finally lost them. Ten minutes later, I was out of breath and sweating as I hid in the back of one of the local restaurants. Between my rapid breaths, I told the host I was being followed. He took me to the back of the restaurant, where I would be obstructed from the view of anyone coming in. I was grateful to have some time to catch my breath.

I had to wait several hours before I left. I was hoping that they would not be waiting at my car for me when I returned to it, and I was relieved to find that they had left. I would have to trade in my car. No doubt they would have documented my vehicle information.

It didn't take long after that initial encounter for the press to find me. The new element of being followed by people who just wanted to get a picture of me was a sudden addition to my daily life. It didn't matter how clever I tried to get to skirt their desire to get pictures of me, they always found me. I tried my best to ignore the attention and go on with my daily life, but it was becoming constant. My hope was that if Atlas and I stayed apart for a little while, then the attention would go away, and the people looking for a story would eventually go away when they thought there was no story for them to find.

As the weeks dragged on, the attention did not abate. I began to wonder if the interest would ever go away. Atlas, Chase, and I stayed in contact with one another through text messages, but it was not the same as being in the same space with one another. Contentions in the world were growing, and wars were popping up that added a new and unique layer of unpredictability to everyday life.

Atlas honored my request to stay away until some of the attention dissipated, but I was now reassessing that request. It was not producing the results I had hoped it would. I hadn't expected it to be this difficult not to be able to see him. I was blanketed by this feeling that the work in both Chase's and Atlas' lives was unfinished. I wanted very much to finish that work for the Lord. I knew the best way for that to happen was to follow the Lord's guidance and to be patient while He laid that path forward.

I needed that path forward more and more with each day that passed.

Atlas

I looked down at my phone at the video footage of Aria being followed to her apartment. I felt a pang of guilt pierce the center of my chest. I had promised her that I could handle the press, and here they were, flooding the internet with her image every day.

It would not stop.

I tried to quell the attention by staying away from her. I tried to go out with friends to see if I could distract the press away from Aria. I went to places I knew they could easily find me. I had felt guilty for asking my friends for the favor of accompanying me, but they were very accommodating and agreed to my request without question. They were used to the extra attention by now.

I still remember the first video that was released. She'd looked right at the camera and spoke my name, and there was something I couldn't quite identify in her eyes as she looked at the camera. There was a message hidden in the depths of the ocean of her eyes that I was having trouble interpreting.

I didn't like being away from her. I didn't like that she was going through the excess attention she had never wanted. I didn't like that I couldn't help ease the burden of this tension.

It finally got to the point where I decided to release an official statement saying that Aria and I were simply friends and nothing more. If this didn't work, then

I wasn't sure what would work. I wanted to be able to honor my promise to her.

All of my plans failed. Not only did the attention not leave her, but the whole situation got more intense than it had been before. No one was convinced that we were merely friends.

I was at a total loss as to what to do now. I got back to my house one evening after a long day of filming reshoots, and I opened the sliding glass door that overlooked the beach. I watched the well-orchestrated dance of the waves against the shore. The beauty of the Pacific Ocean was a difficult thing to capture with words, but I was finding it difficult to appreciate the view in this present moment.

I ran my hand through my hair in frustration. I did the only thing that I could think of as I wrestled with the weight of everything that had taken place since the first night I met Aria. How much things had shifted in my life since that night.

"God. I know it's been a while since I talked to You. I'm sorry it has taken me so long to reach out to You. I don't deserve Your kindness or Your mercy, but I'm asking You to intervene in this situation. Aria doesn't deserve this. She doesn't deserve to go through all of this by herself. I don't know what to do, but I know that if anyone has the answer to this mess, it is You."

I paused as I tried to weigh what was on my heart and put it together in a way that would help put into words the burden that was on my heart.

> "I have struggled with trying to understand how her path even crossed mine, to begin with. I have struggled with letting go of the fact that You would send someone like her into my life to try to help me with the burden of my mother's passing. After so much time spent mourning her loss, it seemed unfathomable to me that You care about me so much that You would reach out to me in my despair in such a way."

I took a deep breath as I felt my chest constrict with the overflow of emotion held captive behind the steel bars of my prison cell of pain. I wiped at the tears on my cheeks as that prison began to gently break apart inside of me. It scared me at first, but I kept praying, and the more I prayed, the more I felt freedom birthing itself inside of me.

> "Please, help her. Please, help me help her. I'm sorry it has taken me until now to reach out to You, but I need You. Aria can't shoulder this weight on her own. I can see it with every new picture that gets published. I can see it with every new video that gets posted on the internet. She's closing in on herself, and I hate the fact that I can't

help her the way she helped me. Please, help me help her."

I went to bed that night with a heavy heart. Nothing was helping, and I was running out of options to try to help her. How do you help someone who is a whole country away?

———————

Aria was walking on sand so light in color that it appeared white. In all the places I had been, I had never seen sand that color before. Her back was facing me as I trailed behind her. Her white dress billowed in the breeze coming in from the ocean. She looked out at the descending sun on the horizon of the ocean.

I tried to increase my pace to get closer to her, but the distance between us seemed to stay the same. I couldn't force myself to get any closer to her. She had a lost look in her eyes as she came to a stop and turned to face the sun. I wanted nothing more than to hug her, but I couldn't get to her, no matter how much I tried.

"Watch."

I turned in every direction to see who had spoken the command, but I found no one.

"Watch."

This time the voice had spoken the word louder.
What was I supposed to watch? I kept my eyes on Aria
as she crossed her arms over her and rubbed away what
I imagined was the chill from the ocean breeze. Her eyes
remained fixed on the horizon.

I watched her eyes soften. The light from the sun re-
flected from the surface of the tear as it streaked down her
cheek. "Please, save them," she spoke softly. Her voice
had been just above a whisper, and I should not have
been able to hear what she had said from this distance
away, but I had heard her spoken plea.

Just as I was about to look out at the horizon to see whatever it was Aria was so focused on, I abruptly awoke from
my dream. It took me a minute to wake up enough to see
what time it was. I groaned as 3:10 a.m. stared back at
me from my phone.

As much as I needed to go back to sleep, I knew that I
would not be able to after having a dream like that. The
dream had felt so real. I remembered how real the breeze
had felt and the unmistakable smell of the salty ocean air.

I remembered the voice I couldn't find the owner
of, and it made the hair on the back of my neck stand.
What was that voice? What had Aria been looking at so
intently? Whatever it was had made that tear fall from
her. Whatever it was had made her voice her plea.

I brewed some coffee and took the few uninterrupted hours I hadn't expected to have to answer e-mails, text messages, and voicemails from the day before. It was the voicemail from someone on my public relations team that I found the most difficult thing to contend with. The press was not buying the friend story.

I dialed Emily's number.

"What do you mean they are not buying the friend story?"

I heard Emily sigh on the other end of the phone. "She's everywhere, Atlas. They are seriously relentless with her. They will not leave her alone," she said and yawned.

"I don't understand. There's literally one picture of me with her. The amount of interest doesn't make sense to me."

There was a pause from the other end of the phone that seemed unlike Emily. I had a funny feeling inside of me that made me think I was missing something. A suspicion I couldn't put words to dawned within me. "Emily... there is only one picture of her and me, right?"

"Uh... about that. Apparently, there is another one," she said in a timid voice that I was very unused to hearing from her.

"What? What is it? Can you send it to me?" She agreed to send me the picture right away, so I put the call on speakerphone while I waited for her to send me the picture through text message.

When I received the picture and opened it, I struggled with trying to understand what it was I was looking at. My apartment in New York City faced Central Park. How had someone gotten a picture inside of my apartment?

There it was. One of the most personal moments of my life had somehow ended up on the internet. I saw Aria's silhouette as she was sleeping next to the couch where I had fallen asleep that first night we met.

This was a public relations catastrophe.

"How was someone able to get a picture like that?"

"Uh... that's not the only one, Atlas. Another one just got posted. Here, I'll send it to you," Emily stated.

This one was taken at the premiere. It was that moment when I first spotted her. My shock was evidenced on my face, but there was also determination there too. Aria was entirely focused on me. Many people who looked at this picture would misunderstand what the reality of that moment was. They would see it and make assumptions without bothering to ask any questions.

Things were about to go from bad to worse for her.

"Cancel the lease for the apartment in New York City. Keep me posted if anything else becomes available. I'll have to stay here for a bit while I figure out what to do next," I said.

"You got it. What about Aria? Do you want us to release a statement?"

I pondered her question and tried to think of a solution that may calm things down, but I was coming up with nothing. It was becoming quite clear that I couldn't protect her while we were both on opposite ends of the country. That didn't leave many options.

"Apart from her moving across the country, I really don't know what else can be done at this point," I replied.

I got a text message from her just then.

ARIA: *Have you seen the pictures?*

ME: *Yes. I am so sorry. I don't know how someone would be able to get a picture inside my apartment.*

ARIA: *Are you okay?*

ME: *Me? Not me. You. Are you okay?*

ARIA: *I've been better. The pressure is starting to wear on me. And yes, you. It must be a weird feeling having your privacy violated like that.*

I stared at her response and found myself once again taken aback by how thoughtful she was for others while so much of her life had been upended just by knowing me. I couldn't remember the last time I had encountered someone like that. I realized I missed her much more than I had stopped to let myself consider.

Emily's voice interrupted my musings.

"You might have an idea there," she said.

What? Wait, what had I said? It took a minute, but I finally remembered. I had mentioned her moving across the country.

"I'm not sure where you're going with that, Emily."

"Think about it. If she was here, then you would have way more influence over how much she is getting harassed right now. You know all of the tricks in how to avoid the paparazzi. You know how to navigate the chaos of being in the public eye constantly. She has no experience with it."

That was a tall order. I couldn't ask her to upend her life by moving across the country. That was far from fair of me to even suggest something like that.

Emily did have a point, though. I knew all of the tricks. I knew how to curb a great deal of the chaos. If I made it clear from a public relations standpoint that Aria and I were close with one another, that would take some of the wind out of the sails of the press. It would have to be somewhat transparent, though. If there was a hint of secretiveness behind it, then the pressure would not yield.

I didn't know that I could ask her to move out here, but I could ask her to visit.

———————

I was in the same dream again. I watched Aria's footsteps. I watched her stop. I watched her turn to face the sun.

I watched that tear make its way down her cheek.
I didn't hear any voice this time.

I tried to turn to look at whatever it was she was looking at as she whispered the same plea she had the first time.

I tried to fight waking up, but I couldn't. It felt like I was being pulled out of the dream. I looked at the time and found 3:10 a.m. staring back at me. Same time. Mostly the same dream. Why was it more difficult to wake up this time?

I didn't know enough about dreams to understand the symbolism and how complex that symbolism could be, so I wasn't well studied on what they could mean. I did know enough to know that it was very unwise to dismiss dreams as though they were inconsequential. The discovery process always added value in ways that other things in life couldn't replicate.

I took the extra time I had and opened my Bible. I knew dreams were significant in Scripture, and I needed to know why. The first person I came across was the account in Genesis where Joseph interpreted Pharaoh's dream. While I found it very helpful, I felt like I was missing something.

I spent some more time searching and came across Daniel. I was left in wonder as I read about his life and how God used him. My research left me with a lot to consider.

I spent the next several days meditating on the contents of the dreams and the possible path forward to help Aria. All of this was distracting me from my work, and it was starting to show in the circles beneath my eyes and the sudden forgetfulness of my lines. I knew it was unprofessional, but I was having trouble finding solutions to the problems.

"Cut," Garrett commanded.

I looked at our director and already knew by the look in his clear blue eyes that he was not pleased. He ran a hand through his short wavy hair and took his gold-rimmed wire-framed glasses off as he put his head in his hand. All the actors on set froze. No one wanted to shoulder the blame for Garrett needing to cut the scene. They didn't need to shoulder any blame, though. It was my burden to bear.

"Okay. We're done for the day. See you all Monday. Remember... 5 a.m., please," Garrett addressed everyone as he stood up to stretch. I smiled at my colleague, and she mouthed the words "good luck" to me. She knew something was off with me and had been nothing but kind and supportive as I had tried to focus on working my stuff out.

"Atlas," Garrett said.

I sighed and walked over to where Garrett stood offset. His blue eyes pierced mine. "I don't know what's going on, man, but you've got to pull yourself together." It had been several years since any director had a conversation like this with me. I took my work seriously and knew how impactful a good story could be for audience members. It always moved me to watch how a film moved others. I had been that person many times myself. I became an actor because I wanted to be a part of bringing impactful stories to life for the audience in a way that could hopefully resonate with people.

I had been that person for Aria.

I felt a pang in my chest. I rubbed at the spot, knowing that I needed to deal with all of this, but still unsure of how to accomplish that. There seemed to be only one path forward, but I didn't know if Aria would agree.

Why was I being so hesitant? This was all becoming so frustrating. I needed to have faith to take that elusive path forward.

"I'm sorry, Garrett."

I rubbed the back of my neck to try to ease some of the built-up tension there. "You know I don't like the fact that I am disrupting the process." I met his eyes and hoped he could see my sincerity.

Garrett sighed and pressed his lips together. "I know. I know you don't intend to disrupt the process. I don't usually ask personal questions, but I feel like maybe I could offer you some help. Is it that woman that's constantly in the press regarding you?"

I nodded in response and winced.

"Seems to me like the reason why you're so distracted is because of what she is going through," Garrett said.

I released a breath with frustration that I made no attempt to hide. "She didn't ask to be thrust into the limelight. She didn't want that. But she was willing to risk it because she knew I needed help."

Garrett nodded in understanding. "Ah. Well, all the way out there, I would imagine she has no idea how to deal with all of the attention. Have you considered flying her out here? If you make a public statement, you may be able to get some control over the chaos."

"I have given that some thought. I want to have her come out here, but I'm not sure she would go for it. She may think that going directly into the lion's den is the wrong way to mitigate the attention," I finished. "I already released one statement, and that backfired big time," I added.

"All you can do is try, Atlas. Look, if it can incentivize things, you can offer to have her come by the set and watch the process firsthand. Maybe it will distract her from the pressures of constantly being followed. If nothing else, it would give her a break from the cameras while she's here hanging out with us."

I smiled my thanks to Garrett. It was no small gift he was offering. "Thank you, Garrett. I'll do that."

I waited until I got to my car to text Aria.

ME: *Will you come out to Los Angeles? I would love to see you. Chase kind of needs to see you. You can even come by the set to check out some of the process of filming if you'd like to see that.*

ARIA: *Let me pray about it.*

I smiled and chuckled to myself. I expected nothing less. I knew I missed her, but I didn't realize just how much I had missed her until that moment.

The dream was different this time. A man stood off to the side of Aria. He was pointing at her.

I couldn't focus on him like I wanted. I wanted to make out his features, but something was prohibiting me from being able to focus on him enough to make out any definable features.

He told me to "watch." Ah, so he had been the voice in the first dream.

I drew my eyebrows together, hoping that he could see my confusion. "Who are you?" I hadn't spoken the words. I had thought the words. But those words had permeated the air around us as though I had spoken them more clearly than I ever could have spoken them from my mouth. How could a thought feel more potent than words spoken out loud?

The air around him changed before my eyes, and it began to thicken. Time seemed inconsequential. Aria wasn't responding to whatever it was that was taking place between the stranger and me.

"I may be a stranger to you, but you are not a stranger to me," came his voice.

I found that statement confusing. I watched as the air around him seemed to blur out as his image changed before my eyes. For some reason, the light behind him started to grow brighter. That didn't make any sense to me. The sun was to my right, and this stranger was standing off to the left of Aria. There shouldn't be a light behind him. Even as I thought that, the light behind him grew brighter. It became so intense and so pure in its color that my eyes became too sensitive, and I was forced to look down. I couldn't take the brilliance of that light anymore.

I felt the man approach me, but I couldn't look up despite my attempt to look up. The light was too bright, and I had to shield my face with my arms.

What was this?

"You need to protect her," came the stranger's voice. It didn't sound the same way as hearing a person speak out loud sounded. It sounded like I was hearing this stranger's thoughts.

"Aria? I don't know how. Who... who are you?"

Everything around the stranger and I began to darken until he was the only source of light. I still had to shield my eyes from the radiance coming from him. I couldn't feel my surroundings any longer. I couldn't make out the structure of the sand on the beach or even hear the sway of the ocean against the sand any longer.

"She will accept your offer. When she does, you must protect her," he said. There was a power in his voice that made me want to kneel before him. "Do not kneel before me. There is only One that deserves the honor of being knelt before. I am but a messenger."

"What kind of messenger?"

The dream was growing stranger by the moment. How was I to know that his intentions were good? How was I to know that I could trust him?

"The kind of messenger that is commissioned by God."

That would mean...

"I'm the angel Gabriel."

How was that possible? Everything in my mind wanted to deny what he had just said. How would something like that even be possible?

I was immediately taken back to what I had read in the Bible about Daniel. I was suddenly very grateful I had done some research into dreams when I had; otherwise, I may not have been prepared for this moment. Daniel had seen Gabriel too.

Why come to me? Surely there are other people that are more important than me.

The air around us grew even thicker, and the temptation to kneel grew stronger. I knew I had to resist that temptation, but I didn't know how to accomplish that.

I managed to find the strength within me, but it took all the willpower I had within me.

"It is the time of the thinning of the veil between earth and heaven. Aria needs you. She will accept your offer. You must protect her. You are stronger together than you are apart. You will need one another in the days ahead."

I felt the air beginning to thin and the light coming from him beginning to dim. I knew my time with him was coming to a close. I had so much more I wanted to talk with him about.

"Wait. Why me?"

"You have more influence than you think. Honor your faith before men, and your Father will honor you in heaven."

I woke up with ease. It felt like I hadn't even been sleeping; that's how easily I came out of the dream. There was no struggle, just an established peace in my heart.

I looked at the time, 3:10 a.m.

I smiled a genuine smile for the first time in a long time. Aria's text displayed on the screen of my phone. She agreed to come out. She needed a week because that was the earliest her work could accommodate her.

I booked her flight and sent her itinerary over to her.

the reunion

I had expected the reoccurring dream to stop after my encounter in the last dream. I was still trying to process everything I had been told in that dream, but I was having a great deal of difficulty doing so, and part of me was wrestling with doubts about the contents of the dream. I knew I shouldn't doubt, but there was that small part of me that kept asking why someone like me would have such an encounter with an angel.

Aria would be arriving the day after tomorrow, and I wanted nothing more than to tell her what had happened, but I wasn't sure how she would take the information. I busied myself with planning for her arrival to make sure everything went off without a hitch. I didn't want her followed anymore. I finally had a plan for that, but that would have to wait until after she safely landed.

When I dreamt that night, it was the similar components of the sand that was nearly white, following her as she walked, watching her as she faced the sun, and seeing that lone tear fall down her cheek.

This time I was permitted to turn to see what she had been so focused on in the dream. I had thought the light had been coming from the setting sun, but as I looked off in the distance, I did not see the familiar circle of the sun. I saw something else. There was a bright light of a figure hovering in the sky in the distance.

I heard her plea again, "Please, save them," and realized she was addressing her plea to the figure hovering in the sky. It occurred to me then that Gabriel had not been pointing at Aria. He had been pointing at the figure in the distance.

What did that mean?

I wasn't used to feeling nervous, but I was feeling nervous as I waited on word from Chase that Aria's plane had arrived on time. I kept checking my phone to see if I had that text from him that I had been eagerly anticipating. There was nothing yet.

Why was I nervous? Honestly, with as much stuff that had taken place since I had last seen her, I could be nervous for any number of reasons. I didn't have a lot of time to ruminate over all of that right now. I focused on my lines as I tried to wrap up for the day. I had already spoken with Garrett about having Aria on set with me tomorrow. He had eagerly agreed.

CHASE: *Landed. Heading your way now.*

I breathed in a deep breath and held it in for a few moments before finally letting it release. I hadn't realized how tense I had been while waiting for her plane to arrive. I knew Chase was still struggling with something, and my hope was that Aria could somehow help him. She had seemed to be able to help him a little bit the last time we had seen one another, and so far, the only one that Chase had opened up to was her.

She had that effect on people.

I smiled as I wrapped up for the day and began the drive home.

A short time after I arrived home, I saw Chase's SUV pulling up the stone driveway. The remaining tension in me evaporated so easily that it seemed like it had never been there to begin with. I opened the door and walked out to greet her as she got out of the passenger side. She smiled at me, and every ounce of the burden she'd been carrying on her own was gone from her eyes. I quickly took in her light blue sweater and blue jeans that were so light they appeared almost white and wondered why she was wearing such thick material when the weather was so warm.

Chase was taking her luggage out of the back of the vehicle as I finally reached her and immediately wrapped her in a hug. "I hope you don't mind," I whispered to her. I heard her chuckle.

"Mind what? Hugs?"

I nodded. "Yeah. Usually, I ask first, but it sort of feels like forever since we have seen one another," I said.

She pulled away to look at me. That smile was still there, and there was a joy that filled her eyes that I had seen absent from her for far too long. Where did that joy come from?

"You seem so happy," I commented as I continued to observe that joy shining from her eyes.

She leaned forward and whispered to me. "I have some good news to share with you." She made a motion toward Chase.

I drew my eyebrows together so she could see my curiosity.

She laughed and pulled away. "Your house is beautiful." That joy in her eyes was replaced by a look of wonder as she looked past me at the Tuscan-style home I had purchased not long ago. I was still trying to get used to the space.

"Thank you. The beach in my backyard kind of sold me on it. It's difficult to say no to a view like this one."

"I can only imagine," she replied.

"Not for long. The sun sets in about an hour. It's yours to take in as you'd like," I said as Chase, Aria, and I walked inside. "So, I have the left side of the house ready for you. I'll be on the right side. I wanted you to feel as comfortable as possible. I hope that is okay."

She nodded as we entered through the front door.

She turned to smile at Chase as we all stood in the entryway of the house. "Chase, is it okay if I tell Atlas?"

My eyes shot to Chase. He was setting her luggage down. He put his hands on his hips as he looked at her. "Tell me what?"

Chase gave Aria a small smile. His eyes turned to meet mine. "Well, I... I'd like to tell you, actually. It took a little longer to get here than normal because I was really struggling with something, and Aria and I pulled over to talk. I know you have told me about Jesus, Atlas, and last time I spoke with Aria, she was telling me about Jesus as well."

My smile was automatic.

"I've really been battling something, and I finally realized that I had two choices. I could keep battling this thing that won't go away, or I could try it His way. So, Aria was gracious with her time, and she helped me give my life to Christ."

That must explain why her eyes were lit with such joy. Tears came to my eyes as I embraced Chase in a tight hug. "I'm so happy for you, Chase. We are here for you every step of the journey."

"Just think," Aria's voice sounded as I pulled away from Chase. "Scripture says that all of heaven rejoices when one who is lost is saved. You have all of heaven rejoicing over you right now, Chase," she finished with nothing but love and joy shining from her eyes.

I took a quick second to thank God for interrupting my life with her presence. There was more to iron out, but I would take this moment to simply be grateful for the work of the Lord in the affairs of mankind.

Chase helped Aria to her room while I set out dinner for us. He stayed to eat with us as we spoke about the life of a believer and how beautiful it is. There was so much for him to look forward to, and it was so exciting to see him at the beginning of his spiritual journey. It was even more amazing to know that we had also gained a brother in Christ for eternity.

As Aria and I watched Chase pull out of the driveway, she sighed gently. "There's nothing more beautiful than seeing someone come to the saving knowledge of Christ," she said. She had her arms wrapped around herself like they had been in that reoccurring dream I had. She turned to smile at me.

I was once again taken aback by her. "You really mean it, don't you," I whispered to her.

Her eyes watered, and a tear fell down her cheek. "There is no greater commission that we have than to tell others about Jesus Christ. To give people the answer to eternal salvation. To give them the answer to the pains of this life. To introduce them to the greatest love we have ever known. Yeah, I really mean it, Atlas. Every single person has a value that we do not determine. That value is established by God and to know that we can play a part in introducing others to Christ is so unspeakably beautiful."

As I watched the tears of joy fall down her cheeks, I realized why it was that Gabriel told me I needed to protect her. People who had a heart like hers easily bore the weight of the world. If that wasn't balanced out with the beautiful things God gave us, then the pain could easily become too heavy of a burden for her to bear.

I took this opportunity to view my name in a different light. Atlas was often depicted as a man carrying the world on his shoulders. There were many opportunities in life to feel that way. Aria had shown up at a time when I couldn't bear the weight of the world, so she bore it for me. Maybe I could do the same for her now.

As we watched the sun set over the Pacific Ocean, I was reminded yet again of the dream I had. I wasn't sure if I should tell her yet, so I kept it to myself for the time being. I watched how serious her expression became as she gazed out at the descending sun.

Her eyes turned to find me already looking at her. "Atlas," she said as she let me see the weight of whatever she was carrying displayed clearly in her eyes. "Something big is about to happen. I don't know what, but I can feel it. It's this awareness that we are standing on the precipice of something big."

I knew it took a lot for her to share that with me. I smiled at her and hugged her again. She felt so much like home to me. I looked at the house I bought not long ago and pondered about how it was that a structure so beautiful had never given me that sense of home, but instead, it was this connection God had clearly orchestrated that gave me that feeling of home.

———————

I watched Aria as she took in everything that Garrett was showing her. She was utterly enthralled by every step in the process of what it meant to direct a film. I laughed as she mimicked Garrett's posture. She probably didn't realize she was doing it, given how focused she was on the screen Garrett was pointing at.

It wasn't long before the rest of the crew gravitated toward her to show her their respective areas of expertise. I watched the sound crew put a headset on her and show her how they positioned the sound boom, and explain why it was done the way it was done. The sound crew even let her hold it in position so she could experience how delicate of a process it could be to hold it in just the right position to pick up the sound properly.

Garrett approached me during lunch. While the other cast members made their way to their trailers, I hung back on set with Garrett. Aria had accepted an invitation from my colleagues to join them for lunch, so it was just Garrett and me.

"She's an interesting one," Garrett said between bites of his sandwich. "Can't quite make out what it is, but she's... different."

I smiled to myself. I knew what it was, but I found it was better for people to discover those things on their own. It was their journey to take. I was simply along for the ride. "Yeah. She's special," I replied.

"Is it true? What all the press says about how you two met?"

I honestly didn't know what the press was saying about how we met. I knew about the pictures, but I hadn't paid attention to the gossip columns. I met Garrett's eyes. "What are they saying?"

"Just that you two met at that premiere you attended in New York City. No one has the details. The pictures are out there, though, and there's definitely something there. Almost like you two already knew each other. Did you know each other?"

I shook my head as I drank some water. "Not quite. We met at that premiere," I replied.

Garrett shook his head as he pondered on something. "Did you get that same feeling from her when you first met her? Like... she's different?"

I chuckled. "You could say that, yes. You're not wrong. She is different."

"I can't put my finger on it," Garrett replied.

"Well, what does it feel like?"

Garrett finished his sandwich as he thought about my question. "I guess the only way I know how to describe it is like there is this peace around her that is kind of contagious. Like you can't help but feel peace, too, because it is obviously so strong in her. She has this genuine sense of wonder about everything she's not familiar with. There's such an innocent quality about that."

We went back to filming shortly after Garrett and I finished our conversation. I could tell that our conversation wasn't far from the front of his thoughts. I had no doubt that by the end of this day, he would start to understand why she was so different. Jesus wasn't just who she believed in or who she had given her life to. Jesus was a part of her life. She invited Him into everything. It wouldn't take long for others to see that.

The wardrobe team stole her away, and for a few hours, I didn't see her. Knowing that team, they were making her try on clothes. Hopefully, they took pictures so I could see what kind of creative ensembles they came up with for her to try on.

By the time the wardrobe team returned her, there were only a few more hours left of filming. She seemed a little tired as she sat in the chair next to Garrett and watched us film the remaining scenes scheduled for today. She gave me a small smile that seemed intended to reassure me. It must have been obvious that I was distracted by her weariness.

I refocused my attention on my lines and got into the headspace of the character. I quickly understood why Garrett felt the way he did. The way she observed her environment was like she was immersing all of herself into the story being told. There was a look of wonder and curiosity that never left her expression as my world became her world.

I was thankful that it was Friday and we were breaking for the weekend.

We finally finished, and I ordered something for us to pick up for dinner. We were in and out of the restaurant before anyone caught on that it was me. We talked about the day and her experience. I found her excitement contagious and felt immediately grateful that I had taken her to the set with me. All of the stress from those weeks of her handling the press alone was gone from her, and she was freer than I could ever remember seeing her. We were back at my house quickly.

I needed to talk to her about Sunday, but I decided it could wait until tomorrow morning. She was clearly very tired, so we sat down on the off-white couch in my living room to eat and watch something I had filmed last year. I wasn't partial to watching my own work because it felt odd watching myself perform, but she had insisted.

I looked over at her as she watched a particularly emotional scene I had filmed. I still remember every element I had drawn from to get the message of this scene to translate just right. I remembered how far away from God I had felt as we filmed this. It was challenging for me to watch it because of how many elements of my own reality I had put into the performance.

She leaned forward as her eyes roamed over the scene. She was seeing something in it.

She rewound the scene after it was finished to watch it from the point it had started. She watched it again. The look in her eyes spoke to her, trying to go deeper and see the unspoken thing she was observing but that she hadn't quite caught hold of yet.

I wondered if this had been her experience when she had watched the movie that day in November that had started all of this many months ago. I had a new appreciation for what her experience had been then as I watched the way she was experiencing this now. I found myself immediately grateful that I had caved to her request to watch this despite how odd it felt to watch myself perform.

She rewound it again. I watched her watch it again. She made a motion with her eyebrows like something she was watching was confusing her.

As she watched me perform the scene again and cry in the scene again, I noticed a hitch in her chest. I hadn't expected her to cry, but that was exactly what happened next. She paused the scene as she wept. I was so thrown off that I forgot I didn't have any tissues on the coffee table. I went to grab a box and gave it to her as she continued to weep.

"I'm so sorry. I didn't mean to cry," she hiccupped as she took a tissue.

"Don't apologize. Can I ask what it was? What made you cry?"

"I don't like seeing that despair in you. I understand what it's like to go through a crisis of faith, but it is difficult to watch that. It felt too real. It looked too real," she finished with a sob.

I hesitated to say anything as I watched her and the way she experienced my performance. "It... there was a lot of it that was real for me," I finally said.

As she assessed me, her tears began to subside. She listened as I continued. "We filmed this last year, many months before you and I met. I had just lost my mother. It shook my entire foundation. So, I poured everything I was going through into that moment."

Her eyes roamed over my face as she absorbed the details of my expression. "Do you feel that despair still?"

I wasn't surprised that she would ask me such a personal question. I wasn't used to being asked questions like that. I thought about how to answer her as I remembered everything that had happened over the course of these months since our paths crossed. "No. No, I don't feel that despair still. I'm grateful for God's intervention. I was very lost when I met you. I was hurting a great deal. I know that there is still some healing for me to do, but I am grateful that I don't have to make that journey alone."

She smiled, and I saw that joy come back into her eyes. She had a genuine joy knowing that I was no longer in that kind of despair. She had a genuine joy that Chase had accepted Jesus as His Lord and Savior. Gabriel's message to me made more and more sense the more I thought about it, and the more time I spent with her.

"I thought after everything you have been going through with the paparazzi that you wouldn't want to remain acquainted with me," I said as I watched her reaction.

She seemed puzzled by my confession. "Why would you think that?"

I shrugged my shoulders as I thought about how best to answer her. "I saw all the pictures. Between those pictures and our conversations, it seemed like it was too heavy of a burden on you. Granted, you were under the pressure of it all by yourself. I'm sorry I couldn't do more. I tried, but nothing I did worked."

She looked away from me, and she thought about what I had said. "Well, you know I don't like the attention. I feel ill-suited for that kind of environment. It was difficult. There were many sleepless nights. There were countless tears. There was a lot of praying."

"I'm so sorry, Aria. With every picture that came out, I could see how the burden on you was getting heavier and heavier. I could see you closing in on yourself."

She looked back at me and was entirely calm as she smiled at me. "You have nothing to apologize for. I don't want you to think I regret anything because I don't. I am a firm believer that everything happens for a reason. I wouldn't change anything. As unpleasant as the attention is, I would always make the same decision to take that train into the city and try to help you."

After everything that happened that night, I still found her honesty and her courage refreshing. I found her joy contagious. She took her faith seriously. I hadn't realized how much I had been missing in fellowship with other believers because I had been so busy with the demands of my career. I loved every part of what I did and had a new appreciation for just how impactful the telling of a story can be for an audience. But, the fellowship of other believers was a treasure I had not sought out for far too long.

There were no connections in my life that were as strong as this one because Jesus was immersed in the center of it. As much as I wanted to wait until tomorrow to tell her, I figured it was probably best if I just told her now. It was becoming a little easier to predict her reactions, and it felt like the right time.

"I hope you didn't make plans for tomorrow," I said coyly.

She chuckled. "What is it, Atlas?"

"I'm having Chase take you shopping tomorrow."

She drew her eyebrows together in confusion as she looked down at what she was wearing. She assessed her light denim jeans and white sweater. "What's wrong with my clothes?"

"Besides the fact that you are wearing a sweater in eighty-degree weather?" I raised an eyebrow at her.

"I wear layers because I get cold easily," she defended.

"In all seriousness... there's nothing wrong with your clothes. I'm having Chase take you shopping for a dress," I said.

The suspicion in her eyes dawned immediately. I filed the suspicion away and continued my train of thought. I watched her reactions closely. "There is an awards show on Sunday, and you are going to attend it with me," I said.

I watched her eyes go wide. I saw the panic spread across her features. She shook her head. "No. No. Atlas, that is going to make the whole paparazzi thing infinitely worse. I can't." She got up off of the couch we'd been sitting on. I watched her pace back and forth in front of the sliding glass door that led out to the beach and the ocean. She was pulling on the edges of the sleeves of her sweater as she paced back and forth.

"Aria, the paparazzi will not leave you alone. I don't know what the fascination is, but even when I made the statement to the public that you are a dear friend to me, it was not enough to quell the interest."

She stopped her pacing and faced me. "And me showing up with you at an awards show is supposed to mitigate the attention?"

I stood up and went over to her. "I don't know whether we can mitigate the attention, but I do know that if I make it clear that you are important to me, then I can help protect you."

She shook her head. "No, that doesn't make sense, Atlas. Think about it. I show up to this with you, and reporters are going to be chomping at the bit to get details…."

I interrupted her. "I can handle the details."

"It's not just that. I don't do well in large crowds unless I know that it is God who wants me there. I'm not built well for the attention. I'm an empathetic person, and when I am in large gatherings, it takes all my energy to get through it. I'm naturally inclined to spot people in pain. Now take one example of that and amplify it by… what a few hundred plus people."

"Then focus on me. Consider me your anchor for the evening," I offered.

She shook her head again. "What happens when I go back home? It's a temporary solution to what is quickly becoming a permanent problem." Her eyes began to shine with tears.

Here was the moment I'd been leading up to. I said a silent prayer hoping that this would not cause her to walk out of my life. I thought back to what Gabriel had said. I knew her well enough to know that all she needed to know was if God was in it, she would follow Him. My hope was that this moment would be one of those moments.

"Then don't go home," I said softly.

Her panic started to wane as she assessed me, and the meaning behind my words began to take shape in her eyes. "Don't go home?" Her confusion was clear as she shaped my statement into a question.

"Stay," I replied.

She looked away from me and out at the ocean as she crossed her arms in front of her. She was so still I could barely make out if she was breathing. I wanted to give her space with her thoughts, but the prolonged silence was making me antsy. Finally, she met my eyes and answered me.

"I will go with you. I trust your judgment. If you say it will help quell the attention, then I am willing to give it a try. This is foreign territory for me, though, so please," she had trouble with the rest of what she was trying to say.

"I will catch you if you fall," I stated. "You have nothing to worry about. I'm not throwing you into the lion's den. I've got this," I assured her.

She nodded. I wished that she would smile again. "As to the other matter," she started. I winced when she called it a "matter." She didn't catch my reaction as she was currently looking at a single spot on the expanse of floor between us. "I'll pray about it. Good night, Atlas," she finished without looking at me.

She left, and I immediately prayed that God would make the stabbing sensation in my chest go away.

the unthinkable

I woke up abruptly from the dream. My heart was racing, and I was having trouble catching my breath. I felt tears flood my eyes as I remembered the dream. I never wanted to dream another dream like that. I never wanted to see Aria like that. I never wanted to feel that feeling of not knowing her. I let myself become resubmerged inside of the contents of the dream.

I stood at the end of the pier, temporarily transfixed by the scene before me. This part of Boston was surprisingly quiet as the city was held in suspense, preparing for the evening rush of people ready to leave work and go home for the day. No lights had yet had the opportunity to click on as darkness had not yet descended upon the tall buildings that made up the iconic Boston skyline.

I walked with my head down to hide my face from any potential passersby. I was thankful that the steady, heavy rain had given me the opportunity to obscure myself from the line of sight of others as I held my black umbrella above me. It was just a pop of color I caught

from my periphery that put a hiccup in my steps. It was so
gray out that even something as soft as the seafoam green
of her sweater was enough to catch the general curiosity
of my gaze.

Normally, I would have briefly looked and kept
walking to my destination, but the scene I caught sight of
temporarily transfixed me.

I stood frozen as I observed. I gripped my umbrella
in my hand to hold it steadier as the wind from the ocean
came in toward me at a steady and firm pace. I put my
hand in the pocket of my black peacoat to shelter my
exposed skin from the dampness of the cool and salty sea
air.

It reminded me of home.

I felt a gentle pang in my chest. It was the pang
that was specific and precise when one contended with
feelings of nostalgia. Had it not been for the rain-soaked
woman currently gripping the rail of the pier as she stood
hunched over, peering into the dark depths of the ocean,
I may have let myself get caught up in that nostalgia that
had reared itself upon me.

But she had caught my attention. Her seafoam green
oversized sweater clung to her slender form as she braced
the rail of the pier like it was the only thing holding her
up. Her hair was short in the back and longer in the
front. Rain drenched the bare exposed skin at the back of

her neck, and her hair fell in front of her face in soaked strands as she stared into the ocean beneath her.

No umbrella. Nothing to protect her from the elements. Her face held no expression, and the longer I observed her, the more I came to realize that she didn't care. Something about that single truth shook my usually steady demeanor.

I began walking down the pier without giving it a second thought. I had intended to deliberately avoid people today as I craved a much-needed moment of peace and silence with myself, but I couldn't walk away from her sad expression and sullen demeanor.

She folded her arms over the rail and rested her head like she was exhausted. I watched her close her eyes, but still no expression. Her face was blank. Her sweater lifted above her denim jeans to expose just a little skin on her back. She didn't even shiver.

I finally reached her spot at the end of the pier. She didn't look up once. It seemed odd to me that she hadn't heard me approach, but maybe the waves of the unsettled ocean had drowned out my footfalls.

I stopped several feet away from her and gently cleared my throat to avoid startling her. Was she aware enough not to be startled by an approaching person? I wasn't so sure of the answer to that question but noticed she made no motion to turn and face me.

"Excuse me," I spoke up above the noise of the wind, rain, and waves of the ocean. She stood up, her back straight as an arrow, and turned to face me. The wet tendrils of her hair came to land against her cheek, where they clung. Was she crying? I couldn't tell with all the rain falling against her skin.

I saw the knowledge reflected in her eyes the moment she knew who I was. I wasn't expecting her to go ridged and take a startled step back.

No one ever did that when they recognized me.

Fear lit up her already bright blue eyes, and I re-actively drew my eyebrows together in confusion. "You know me?" I asked it as a rhetorical question and meant it more as a statement, but she replied anyway. "How could I know you when I don't know you?"

What?

That was a curious way to answer me when I could clearly see the look of recognition in her eyes. "But... you know of me," I said. She looked confused and mildly agitated. At least I could now observe some emotion from her instead of that eerie blank expression that had so propelled me to approach her.

"Why do people say that? I don't know you. Does anyone ever truly know another individual, or do we just trick ourselves into believing that we do?"

Ah. She was one of those types of people. Her solitude on the pier was beginning to make more sense now. However, her sadness remained a mystery, as did her lack of proper protection from the elements.

I took a step forward, and she immediately responded with a step back. Her eyes held panic as she focused on me and my movements. Why was she so skittish?

"I won't hurt you. You have nothing to fear," I tried to ease her obvious apprehension of me.

She chuckled, and it seemed to have a sarcastic edge to it. She looked out to the ocean where she had been staring before. "Maybe you won't hurt me, but you couldn't possibly guarantee that I have nothing to fear." I watched her upper body jerk back just slightly as she moved. She squeezed her eyes closed as she turned back to me and took a measured breath. "I recognize you," she stated softly.

I was beginning to understand she had an appreciation for the precision of words. "People don't usually respond to me the way you did when you initially saw me," I observed.

She opened her eyes to pierce me with her gaze. "I'm not the type to chase you down and ask you for your picture if that's what you mean. Don't you crave peace from time to time?"

I was startled by her response, but I was too preoc-
cupied with the fact that she was still unfazed by her exposure to the elements. "Please, come under the umbrella
with me. You must be cold." She eyed me like I was the
last person on the planet that she could ever see herself
trusting. "I won't hurt you," I tried to assure her.

"What does it matter at this point? I've been standing out here for an hour. The rain hasn't bothered me
yet," she said as she closed her eyes and lifted her face to
the heavy droplets falling from the dark gray clouds.

I moved in quickly so she would only have time
to accept the coverage of the umbrella as opposed to
reacting to my sudden approach. She looked at me with
a startled expression as she crossed her arms over her
middle and her lips parted. She looked at my shoulder.
Her expression spoke of how unsure of me she was. She
was clearly mentally retreating to a place where she felt
safe.

I watched her step back a little but not remove herself
from the shelter of the umbrella. I took the small victory.
"Tell me, where are you staying? I will walk you." I made
her the offer as I tried to get her to look at me by searching her face until she lifted her eyes to mine.

She didn't answer me right away. "You sound different than you sound in your movies," she observed.

I leaned in closer. "Sound is amplified in movies," I replied.

"I've seen some of your interviews. It still sounds different in person," she observed. She left me feeling utterly perplexed.

"Why are you out here by yourself?"

"Why did you approach me?"

"You seemed sad, and I... I didn't want you to be sad or... alone," I noted. I reached out to brush the wet strands of her hair away from her cheek, so I could now see her face fully. She jerked back at my touch. She winced and tried to muffle a groan. "You're in pain," I stated as her eyes eventually found mine again. I only had a split second of visual confirmation of my stated observation before her blank expression returned.

"Aren't we all in a measure of pain at one point or another in our lives?"

"You're in a measure of pain right now," I retorted. That blank expression remained on her face. "You do know that that matters, right?" I kept my eyes on her and hoped that I was clearly conveying my confusion at her lack of care for herself.

She looked away and down at the planks of the rain-soaked pier just past where I stood. "You seem kind, Atlas. But kindness is rarely a permanent fixture in my life."

She moved to go past me, but I stopped her with a hand on her upper arm. She was cold to my touch.

That one truth motivated my next action. I took out my phone and pulled up my contact for James. I held her as she looked back at me with that blank expression that was beginning to bother me. I held the phone to my ear. "James. Yeah, I'm ready for that lift. End of pier 7. Okay. See you in a minute."

She looked away from me and yanked her arm away from my grasp. "Thank you for the umbrella," she said as she started to move away.

"Wait. Come with me," I said. I saw her wince as she moved again, and I wanted to know why. She was too guarded for me to just ask her, though. "Please," I said softly.

She turned back to look at me. "Why?" Her expression was a mixture of confusion and frustration, and I found that I much preferred that over the blank one that she wore in times when she clearly should show visible signs of emotion.

"You're cold. I have a place where you can change." She eyed me with skepticism. "Please," I said again.

I don't know why because she had no reason to, but she gave me a slow nod of agreement. I felt pressure leave me, and I absentmindedly noted that I hadn't been aware of the presence of that pressure until this moment.

I saw the black car with tinted windows slowly pull up to the end of the pier. I nodded toward our ride and released her arm as we walked down the pier together. She held her arms, and I knew she was finally feeling the effects of the prolonged exposure to the elements.

I held the umbrella over her as I opened the car door, and she climbed in. I climbed in behind her and settled in. "All good, James, thank you." James nodded at me and pulled away from the curb. When I turned to her, she wore a look of curiosity, and there was an innocence to the expression that kept my eyes on her. "What is it?"

She lifted her arm away from herself and rose it slowly. She was clearly apprehensive, and I found her open vulnerability transfixing.

She ran her hand over the droplets that had landed on my hair when I had collapsed my umbrella to get into the car. She took her hand away when she was finished and folded her arm back into herself. She looked away.

I sat there next to her, completely stunned. She was drenched to the bone, but she had only considered that I had gotten rain on me.

Who was this woman?

I stared back at my reflection in the mirror in my bathroom. That dream shook me. It also revealed to me how much her presence in my life mattered. I pondered the meaning behind all of it. Maybe my presence in her life mattered more than I realized. If our paths had never crossed, would she be like she had been in the dream?

It seemed so unthinkable that it was hard to imagine Aria ever being in a state where she didn't have that joy I was so used to seeing in her now. Deep within me, I knew I was being shown what would have become of her had our paths never intersected. I didn't like what I saw. There had been so much defensiveness in her in that dream. I found myself so grateful that God had worked on her behalf and on my behalf to bring us into the freedom that could only be found in Him.

It amazed me how the Creator of the universe was so deeply immersed in the everyday affairs of mankind. So many people I had encountered thought of Him as absent from the affairs of mankind. My experience was entirely different from that. God had proven over and over to me that He was deeply invested in everything that went on in every given moment.

I was ready for a day of catching up on e-mails and phone calls as I stared back at my reflection in the mirror. Aria had already left with Chase to go shopping. She hadn't let me know she was leaving. I knew it wasn't a personal slight against me, but it felt that way. I knew her well enough to know that she was taking it all very seriously and trying to hear from the Lord regarding what she should do.

I thought about the version of her from my dream and the reality of her now. They seemed like two entirely different people. I suppose that was true in a way. Being lost and away from God had an incredibly lonely feeling that I wouldn't wish upon anyone. I'd been that person once in my life. Knowing what I know now and having the relationship I had with Him now was very much like being a new person. The old person was gone, and the new person remained.

I went from darkness to light.

From fear to faith.

From despair to hope.

From resentment to love.

I never wanted to go back to what I was before. I was so grateful Aria was not the version of herself that I had dreamt about. This is what a redeemed life with Jesus at the center of it all promised. If what we were given was just eternal salvation, that would be enough, but it was so much more than eternal salvation. It was full of blessings and redemption. It was full of freedom and hope. It was full of joy and love beyond our ability to fully understand, but worth every effort to attempt to understand better.

I had wanted to go with Aria, but I also understood her need for some separation, so she could seek the Lord about what it was I was asking of her. My hope was that no paparazzi would catch word of her presence here in town. If they got pictures of her and Chase, the gossip columns would be running amuck with speculation that held no basis in any truth. I didn't want that for her.

I looked down at my phone as a text came in from Garrett.

GARRETT: *It's Jesus, isn't it? Is that what's different about her?*

I smiled as I read his message. She lived her life for Christ, and people around her could pick up on the difference in her, whether she intended to be transparent or not. All it took was one genuine look at her to see that something was different about her.

I remembered that night in New York City when I had looked up and saw her. The second I saw her, I remembered the reoccurring dreams, but the look she had was not like anything I was used to seeing in my life. All it took was one moment of God's intervention, and it changed the course of both of our lives.

ME: *Yes.*

GARRETT: *It makes me think everything I have thought about Jesus isn't true at all.*

ME: *What do you mean?*

GARRETT: *I've always kind of judged Him, I guess. But looking at how she interacts with everyone has me thinking I have seriously misjudged who Jesus is.*

My smile got wider as I watched my director change right in front of my eyes. I thanked God for the work He was doing and for the privilege of being able to see a heart in the process of changing. There was something so indescribably beautiful in seeing someone learn the truth about Jesus.

I thought about the cross and everything Jesus sacrificed so we could find redemption with the Father. From the beginning of time, God was there, working things in such a precise way that no plan or scheme from the enemy could hinder His great works. I admit I didn't fully understand that kind of love, but I was inexplicably drawn to that love.

"Thank you, Father. Thank you for everything You have done. Thank you for everything You are doing, even in this very unpredictable world. Thank you for showing me how much You love me by not letting me stay in that place of despair after my mom came home to You. I admit that I miss her very much, but without You intervening the way You did, I would not have remembered the truth. This is not the life. All of this leads back to You. All of this brings us back to You. I am grateful for everything You have done. Thank you for loving me when I didn't know how to love myself. Thank you for showing me my worth when I wrestled with trying to understand my own worth. I'm Yours forever."

the event

Aria stood in the hallway. We were getting ready to leave for the awards show. I hadn't seen her come back after shopping with Chase. I had some business to attend to this morning, and Chase had asked her to help him minister to a friend of his who really needed help, so she had left with him before I had even woken up this morning.

This was the first time I was seeing her since our conversation the other night when I'd suggested she stay here and not go back.

I smiled softly as I stood there waiting for her to give me insight into what she was thinking. She looked elegant in a dress that was fitted in the bodice and capped sleeves that hugged her shoulders. The skirt of the dress was full and folded in against itself. Not many people risked wearing white to award shows like this, but that is what she had chosen. The beading on the bodice was intricate and made the dress appear to be a unique blending of silver and white. Silver threading was detailed throughout the skirt. Her beaded heels seemed to compliment the beading detail on the bodice of the dress.

She had a sheer white shawl wrapped around her like a loose scarf.

I picked a dark blue suit with a white vest, shirt, and tie. It would complement the style she had chosen well.

We were silent as we walked out to meet Chase, where he waited in the SUV. I waited until we were comfortably settled before striking up a conversation. I wasn't entirely sure what to lead with, but I thought it best to go the safe route.

"How did it go with Chase's friend?"

She considered my question carefully. "Very well, actually. He was very receptive to the Gospel." She smiled, and that unmistakable joy lit up her eyes.

"He accepted Jesus?"

She nodded.

Her smile fell away. "I'm sorry, Atlas. I apologize for the way I responded the other night. It's a big thing that you are suggesting by suggesting I stay out here."

I nodded. "I know." I waited patiently for her to continue. If she hadn't wanted to talk about it, then she wouldn't have opened the door to talk about it. I wanted to give her space to say what she had to say.

"I'm still waiting on direction from the Lord. I hope you can understand why I need that," she finally said.

"I wouldn't expect any different. You need to honor what He would have you do," I replied.

She smiled at me. "So, how bad is this going to be for me? Should I expect to have a panic attack?"

I laughed. "Just let me lead you on this. You just focus on being you. People need to see you for who you really are and not what the columns have been publishing."

There was a whirlwind of action as we pulled up behind the line of vehicles that were parked and waiting for people to exit and make their way down the red carpet. Aria started fidgeting in her seat next to me. I took her hand and held it. She looked at me with a question in her eyes.

"Trust me," I nodded at her waiting for her response to me. She finally pressed her lips together and nodded back at me.

Our vehicle inched its way forward slowly as, one by one, actors and actresses made their exit from their vehicles and down the red carpet. The brush obscured much of our visibility, so all we could currently see was the beginning where the red carpet started.

"I don't belong here," she said in a huff of breath. I could feel her hand shaking as I continued to hold it. She closed her eyes tightly as if it all would somehow go away when she opened them again.

We came to a stop.

It was our turn to make our exit. "Open your eyes and look at me," I instructed her. She finally did as I instructed her. "I've got you." I could see the fear lacing her eyes, but she nodded in agreement despite that fear she was contending with.

When we got out, we were immediately met with an array of flashing cameras and screams from fans who were sectioned off on one side of the red carpet. The other side was a backdrop for pictures. Interviewers were in front of the crowd already in the middle of their interviews.

I looked at Aria to check on how she was responding, and she wore a blank expression as she looked at everything with wide eyes. The shaking in her hand didn't subside, so I repositioned her so her arm was locked on mine. I felt her grip my forearm. It seemed to be helping her anchor herself.

I led her over to the fan section as fans screamed my name. Aria's tension eased as I broke away to sign autographs and take pictures with fans. There were so many, and I always tried to accommodate as many fan requests as I could. In all the excitement, there were times when people got too caught up in the energy of these events and forgot to be respectful of one another as they vied to get a moment with the people that had so inspired them.

When I looked back at Aria to check on how she was holding up, I was both surprised and relieved to find her quietly observing me as I interacted with the fans. She was smiling with that joy in her eyes again.

Someone called out her name, and she looked in the direction it had come from. I walked over to her to check in with her. "Are you okay?"

She nodded. "Absolutely. I have always loved how you interact with your fans. You have never treated them as lesser than you are. You always treat people with the value they deserve," she finished.

She didn't know how much what she said meant to me.

I squeezed her hand and went back to the crowd to sign more autographs and take more pictures. I spent time asking some questions of people and joking with them until I was asked to move along by the attending security personnel. I waved at everyone and blew them a kiss, and took a bow as I thanked them for being here and taking this amazing journey with me.

The first interview was a bit of a rocky one. The person doing the interview began by asking about my relationship with Aria. I attempted to redirect the interview by talking about how lovely the evening was for a celebration of such talented artists. The interviewer didn't seem to be interested in that in this particular moment. In her follow-up question, she asked if Aria's presence here meant that we were a couple.

I didn't normally walk away because I didn't want to come off as rude, but I gently pulled Aria away and let someone else take our spot. I pulled her toward the red carpet and waved at the fans in the background.

Aria's eyes landed on me. "Don't you have other interviews you need to do?"

I shook my head. "No. I'm not nominated for anything, so I don't have the same type of obligations as the nominees would have. I'm just here to show support and maybe insert a little Jesus into all of this energy." I smiled at her and hoped that she could see my sincerity.

"Let's try one more time with an interview," she suggested as she smiled. I found the kindness in her eyes contagious. I nodded and led us to an interviewer who I was confident would be a little more reserved with questions.

"Beautiful night to celebrate, don't you think, Atlas?" Sarah worked for an online company that I was familiar with, and she tended to be much more level when it came to the way she conducted her interviews.

Aria's eyes remained on me as she tried to ignore the cameras. Her arm remained locked on my arm. "Yes, it is absolutely beautiful. It's always a pleasure to get to interact with fans. We're here because of them," I responded to Sarah.

"There's been a lot of rumors going around about the nature of your relationship with Aria. Is there anything you want to say regarding the speculation?"

I looked at Aria and smiled. Her eyes remained on mine, and I was grateful for her confidence in my ability to handle this situation. "As I have stated publicly, Aria is a dear friend of mine." I looked back at Sarah as she waited for me to elaborate further. "I think the scrutiny has been a bit unwarranted, but I can understand why people are interested. Sometimes the best things in life can't be measured. They hold more meaning than we can properly describe."

I watched the confusion on Sarah's face as she tried to understand what the meaning was behind what I was saying.

"Aria, what do you think about what Atlas said?"

Aria searched my face before responding to Sarah's question. She finally looked back at Sarah. "I think sometimes we have a habit of rushing to define something we are still in the process of trying to gain a better understanding about. God's handiwork displayed in the intricacy of the universe should serve as an example of the benefit of seeking better understanding as opposed to rushing to define something we don't have a full understanding about."

Sarah was so stunned she seemed to not know what else to ask.

Aria and I moved forward down the red carpet and stopped for a few more interviews along the way. Those interviews played out much the same as the interview we did with Sarah. I locked Aria's arm on mine and smiled, knowing that she always found confidence in the truest part of herself. Every time she spoke of God or Jesus or the Holy Spirit, the confidence just naturally came.

I spent time introducing Aria to some of my colleagues I had worked with in the past. In some crowds, she seemed more natural than in other crowds. She absorbed all the information I shared with her from a posture of trying to better understand everything that was so new to her.

She had difficulty being around some people, and with others, she gracefully entered into deep conversations with ease. It was difficult to pull her away from those conversations as I could see how much she enjoyed doing a deeper dive into the meaningful things in life. We parted our company with a few more contacts added to Aria's phone and promises made of getting together to continue conversations that had been started tonight.

As we took our seats and the lights lowered, she leaned a little closer to me. She watched with curiosity at the process. "It's rather overwhelming," she whispered to me.

I smiled. "It took me some time to get a little more comfortable with the process. It is a lot of energy in one place."

Halfway through the show, I looked over at her. She looked like she was on the verge of tears. "What is it, Aria?"

She gave me a forced smile. "I oftentimes wonder how many people don't know Him." She sniffled. "That was me once. My heart breaks for the lost," she whispered.

A strange vibration sounded in the room. It took me a moment to realize where the vibration had come from.

Cell phones.

I drew my eyebrows together in confusion. I saw Aria's disposition change from somber to alert. She immediately reached into her purse to check her phone. "Oh my God," she whispered. Her eyes went wide as she covered her mouth in shock.

My internal alarm went off. If Aria was shocked, it had to be significant. She hadn't been shocked by anything up until this moment. She'd been attacked in New York City and still managed to maintain a calm disposition.

Gasps sounded around me as I saw more and more of my colleagues in the audience looking at their phones. I turned my attention back to Aria. "What is it? What happened?"

"We need to go, Atlas. We need to go now," she said as her eyes finally met mine. I didn't ask any more questions. I stood up and moved to get us out of there.

I didn't even have to dial Chase's number to arrange for him to come and pick us up. Chase was there waiting for us as we rushed outside. People were starting to leave as the weight of whatever had taken place began to upend the awards event.

I saw people crying and hugging one another as people were getting frustrated trying to arrange to leave. Many people were on their phones saying they needed to get a hold of a loved one. Whatever had taken place had to be serious.

Aria and I found Chase quickly and were able to leave without incident. As Chase pulled away from the curb, I looked back as people started to rush outside. The look of fear was in the eyes of every person I observed.

"Aria, what happened?"

Aria was crying now, and she tried to hold back her sobs with her hand over her mouth. I looked at Chase. He seemed to be holding back whatever emotions he was warring with. I had left my phone at my house, so I waited patiently for Aria to calm down so she could explain to me what had happened.

"Damascus has been destroyed," she whispered. Tears fell effortlessly from her eyes as she waited for the meaning to take root in me. "The Isaiah 17:1 prophecy has been fulfilled," she whispered as she wept further.

"I'm not familiar with that part of Scripture. Does it tell of the destruction of Damascus? Where is that?"

She nodded. "Yes, it tells of the destruction of Damascus. It's located in Syria. Syria is directly to the north of Israel. It's not just that, Atlas," she whispered.

"What? What else is it?"

She turned her phone to me so I could see the video footage she was seeing. I stared at the footage of Damascus being completely leveled by a weapon of warfare that I had no idea could even exist. I didn't want to even think about the devastation.

I felt a tear fall from my eye.

The next image I saw was of Israel. Flashes from various parts of the nation played out across the screen of her phone. The nation was surrounded. The armies around her were too many to number.

"Ezekiel 38," Aria spoke softly.

I wasn't familiar enough with prophecy to know what Ezekiel 38 spoke about. I shook my head as she watched my reaction.

She put her phone down as she explained what was happening. "Ezekiel 38 speaks of many nations coming against Israel to take from them. Israel will be surrounded by her enemies. God Himself intervenes on behalf of the nation." She showed me the images again. There were images of flags from countries I was not familiar with that were displayed on the military equipment.

We pulled into my driveway a short time later. Aria gave Chase a tight hug and told him to be ready. I didn't know what she was speaking about. She seemed calmer and more focused now. She seemed sure of what she was saying.

We both went inside to change quickly so we could turn on the television to follow what was happening.

I was reminded of Aria's words to me when she said something big was coming. She hadn't been able to put words to the feeling she had. I wondered if this was the big thing.

We watched footage of the armies surrounding Israel. They encamped around the nation and made no immediate move to invade. I wasn't sure if they were aiming for psychological warfare, but it sure seemed that way to me.

We tried to stay awake, but soon the stress of what we were witnessing became too much of a burden. I watched Aria's eyelids as they grew heavy. I grabbed a soft ivory blanket and covered her with it as she finally caved to the demand for sleep. I fell asleep as I watched and waited for whatever was going to happen next to transpire.

the intervention

Aria

*I was dreaming. I was looking over at Atlas as we stood
on the beach in his backyard. I had just stopped walking
along the shoreline. I had turned to face what I thought
was the setting sun. The light was so brilliant. I was
wearing a flowing white dress, and Atlas was wearing
khaki pants and a white linen shirt.*

*"Aria," came a voice that spoke my name directly
behind me.*

*I turned to face the origins of that voice. I could
make out a shape that seemed like it was the shape of a
human, but I couldn't make out any details. Somehow
the person was veiled in such a way that his image was
blurry to me. There was a light behind him that illuminated his shape and began to grow brighter in its
intensity.*

I held my arms up to cover my face as my eyes
couldn't handle the growing light. Where was the light
coming from? I didn't understand what was happening.

"Are you ready?" he whispered.

"Ready? Ready for what?"

"It'll be okay. Everything is about to change," he
whispered.

I gasped as I abruptly woke up. Atlas was sleeping on the couch next to me. I hadn't been aware that I had fallen asleep. It was still dark out. The television showed Israel actively being attacked. A fissure formed on the ground as the camera angled to show an earthquake actively taking place. Buildings shook, and cracks appeared in their structures. Off on the side of the screen was the earlier footage of what had happened in Damascus.

I checked the time, 3:10 a.m.

I sat up and cried. I realized the moment I saw the breaking news on my phone what these events meant on a bigger scale. I realized the prophetic implications. My heart hurt for the world and what it was about to go through. The whole world was standing at the door of everything that the Book of Revelation spoke about. Part of me was filled with the joy of the expectation of seeing our King, and part of me longed for the lost to be saved.

Atlas stirred and saw me crying. He immediately hugged me. Several minutes passed, and he continued to comfort me as we watched the news unfold.

Flashes of unexplainable light repeatedly went across the screen, making it difficult to discern where the light was originating from.

"Are they missiles?"

I shook my head at Atlas' question. "No. Missiles are not that bright. Whatever it is, they are preventing the armies from complete invasion."

"Is it possible they are...." Atlas left his sentence unfinished as his suggestion lingered between us.

"With God, all things are possible. I've never seen light that bright except while dreaming. It certainly could be angels."

Atlas watched me for my reaction. "They are moving so fast. It makes me think there must be hundreds of them." He waited for me to voice my thoughts to his interpretation of what we were both witnessing play out across the screen of the television.

"Walk with me outside?"

Atlas nodded in agreement. We both took a private moment before we ventured out to the shoreline. It felt like the weight of the world was on our shoulders. I took a moment to explain to Atlas what these events meant. As we stood there and looked up at the stars, there was great comfort in knowing that we had fellowship with one another, and the comfort that brought was something the world couldn't duplicate. It brought with it a unique peace that was a gift from God when life took unexpected turns that uprooted our lives.

Sometimes, uprooting things was the only way something new could be planted. Something that would produce greater fruit than we could ever hope for or come up with on our own. The process of transition rarely transpired without a good amount of shaking taking place during the transition itself.

I looked down at my phone and watched unthinkable scenes play out in Israel. These were the things in the Bible I had studied for many years. They were happening now.

It was 3:33 a.m.

"What is that?"

Atlas' question drew my attention away from my phone. I put the phone away as I looked up at something he was pointing at in the sky. It was brighter than any star.

"Is that a comet? Or an asteroid?"

I looked closer as a kind of peace I had never experienced before took root deep inside of me. The light was growing brighter. I realized then that it was approaching the earth.

I looked at Atlas and smiled. "No. No, it's not. Everything's about to change," I whispered. I looked back at that light that I could now see enough of to make out a figure. "Please, save them," I whispered to Him.

"Oh my God," Atlas gasped as he realized what was happening. "Could it be?" Atlas wrapped his arms around me as I watched his shock spread across his face.

"Yes," I whispered. "Not only could it be, but it is."

The edges of his mouth turned down with sadness, but I knew he wasn't sad. "I've waited so long for this moment," he whispered as tears fell from his eyes without effort.

Atlas turned to me with fresh tears shining in his eyes. "Thank you for listening to His call on your heart. I wouldn't be here if you hadn't listened to Him," he said.

I smiled at Atlas and hoped he could see the joy in my eyes. "Are you ready to meet our King?"

A voice like a trumpet saturated the air all around us as we both looked at the light that grew too bright for us to gaze upon directly. The appointed time had finally come.

This was the time of our reunion with the King of Kings and the Lord of Lords, Jesus Christ.

afterword

One day, very soon, we will see the return of our King Jesus. Until that day, no matter what life brings, we have the blueprint given to us in the Bible about how to navigate the changes life brings. We build our house upon the rock of Jesus Christ, knowing that He is our sure foundation.

It is my prayer that this story has highlighted how important all acts of obedience to God are. When we let Him lead us and guide us, all things are possible. He gives us grace in tasks that we may find impossible. He gives us mercy when we make mistakes. He gives us compassion when the pains and frustrations of life may be a little too heavy for us to carry on our own.

His love is as eternal as He is, and when we choose to operate inside of that, then exceptionally beautiful and powerful things happen. His love changes even the most extreme circumstances. His love blesses others who need to feel it and experience it for themselves.

I pray this over the body of Christ: may we exhort one another, may we edify one another, may we uplift one another, may we encourage one another, and may we always love one another the way Christ taught us to love one another. May we be pillars of truth, grace, and mercy. And may the heart of the Father reflect in the eyes of each believer as the world needs to see that light shining in the darkness. In the matchless name of Jesus Christ, I pray this. Amen and Amen!

If you are not a believer and you are reading this, I pray that you may receive the truth about who the Lord is and who He has always been. I pray that you encounter His love in such a way that from that moment until forever, you will be complete. You are found in Christ. You know who you are and who God has called you to be when you learn who Christ is and accept Him as Lord and Savior of your life and seek Him with your whole heart. May now be that time for you. Amen.

appendix one

Hope for the Hurting Heart

For God so loved the world that He gave His only begotten Son, that whoever believes in Him should not perish but have everlasting life. For God did not send His Son into the world to condemn the world, but that the world through Him might be saved.

— John 3:16–17 (NKJV)

Love suffers long and is kind; love does not envy; love does not parade itself, is not puffed up; does not behave rudely, does not seek its own, is not provoked, thinks no evil; does not rejoice in iniquity, but rejoices in the truth; bears all things, believes all things, hopes all things, endures all things.

— I Corinthians 13:4–7 (NKJV)

For we do not have a High Priest who cannot sympathize with our weaknesses, but was in all points tempted as we are, yet without sin. Let us therefore come boldly to the throne of grace, that we may obtain mercy and find grace to help in time of need.

— Hebrews 4:15–16 (NKJV)

Therefore submit to God. Resist the devil and he will flee from you. Draw near to God and He will draw near to you.

—James 4:7–8 (NKJV)

By this we know love, because He laid down His life for us.

— 1 John 3:16 (NKJV)

Beloved, let us love one another, for love is of God; and everyone who loves is born of God and knows God.

— 1 John 4:7 (NKJV)

Now this is the confidence that we have in Him, that if we ask anything according to His will, He hears us. And if we know that He hears us, whatever we ask, we know that we have the petitions that we have asked of Him.

— 1 John 5:14–15 (NKJV)

But He was wounded for our transgressions, He was bruised for our iniquities; the chastisement for our peace was upon Him, And by His stripes we are healed.

— Isaiah 53:5 (NKJV)

a p p e n d i x t w o

Wisdom and Strength

"But You, O Lord, are a shield for me, My glory and the One who lifts up my head."

— Psalm 3:3 (NKJV)

"Preserve me, O God, for in You I put my trust."

— Psalm 16:1 (NKJV)

"I sought the Lord, and He heard me, And delivered me from all my fears."

— Psalm 34:4 (NKJV)

"The eyes of the Lord are on the righteous, And His ears are open to their cry."

— Psalm 34:15 (NKJV)

"The righteous cry out, and the Lord hears, And de-livers them out of all their troubles. The Lord is near to those who have a broken heart, And saves such as have a contrite spirit."

— Psalm 34:17–18 (NKJV)

For the LORD gives wisdom; From His mouth come knowledge and understanding; He stores up sound wisdom for the upright; He is a shield to those who walk uprightly; He guards the paths of justice, And preserves the way of His saints.

— Proverbs 2:6–8 (NKJV)

Keep your heart with all diligence, For out of it spring the issues of life.

— Proverbs 4:23 (NKJV)

Jesus said to him, "'You shall love the LORD your God with all your heart, with all your soul, and with all your mind.' This is the first and great commandment. And the second is like it: 'You shall love your neighbor as yourself.' On these two commandments hang all the Law and the Prophets."

— Matthew 22:37–40 (NKJV)

"Blessed are the poor in spirit, For theirs is the kingdom of heaven. Blessed are those who mourn, For they shall be comforted. Blessed are the meek, For they shall inherit the earth. Blessed are those who hunger and thirst for righteousness, For they shall be filled. Blessed are the merciful, For they shall obtain mercy. Blessed are the pure in heart, For they shall see God. Blessed are the peacemakers, For they shall be called sons of God. Blessed are those who are persecuted for righteousness' sake, For theirs is the kingdom of heaven."

— Matthew 5:3–10 (NKJV)

"Come to Me, all you who labor and are heavy laden, and I will give you rest. Take My yoke upon you and learn from Me, for I am gentle and lowly in heart, and you will find rest for your souls. For My yoke is easy and My burden is light."

— Matthew 11:28–30 (NKJV)

Finally, my brethren, be strong in the Lord and in the power of His might. Put on the whole armor of God, that you may be able to stand against the wiles of the devil. For we do not wrestle against flesh and blood, but against principalities, against powers, against the rulers of the darkness of this age, against spiritual hosts of wickedness in the heavenly places. Therefore take up the whole *armor of God, that you may be able to withstand in the evil day, and having done all, to stand.*

— Ephesians 6:10–13 (NKJV)

about the author

Rebecca Branch has an enduring passion for seeking the deeper aspects of the love of God. One of the greatest pursuits of her walk with the Lord is to pursue a deeper understanding of the facets of the heart of God and to share that with others. She is very much looking forward to the return of King Jesus, but until that day, she is focused on being busy with the Father's work and occupying until He returns.

CPSIA information can be obtained
at www.ICGtesting.com
Printed in the USA
BVHW070553150223
658552BV00009B/185

9 798887 384290